"Why do you sa[...] women around, [...] the first chance you get?"

"She was crying. I wanted you to be able to finish your shower," Frisco said defensively. "I didn't know Emmie would fall asleep on me. Now I don't want her awakened, because she'll start crying again. What's wrong with that?"

"Nothing. I just wonder why you're working so hard to be tough when you've got a soft heart."

Frisco snorted. "No one says I've got a soft heart."

"You're letting me sleep in your room."

"You made yourself at home!"

Annabelle smiled. "I think you're more softhearted than you care for anyone to know."

Frisco didn't like this little lady looking at him so directly. Her big eyes took him in as if she knew him. Annabelle was getting to him. Tomorrow she had to go.

Dear Reader,

This month Harlequin American Romance delivers favorite authors and irresistible stories of heart, home and happiness that are sure to leave you smiling.

COWBOYS BY THE DOZEN, Tina Leonard's new family-connected miniseries, premieres this month with *Frisco Joe's Fiancée,* in which a single mother and her daughter give a hard-riding, heartbreaking cowboy second thoughts about bachelorhood.

Next, in *Prognosis: A Baby? Maybe,* the latest book in Jacqueline Diamond's THE BABIES OF DOCTORS CIRCLE miniseries, a playboy doctor's paternal instincts and suspicions are aroused when he sees a baby girl with the woman who had shared a night of passion with him. Was this child his? THE HARTWELL HOPE CHESTS, Rita Herron's delightful series, resumes with *Have Cowboy, Need Cupid,* in which a city girl suddenly starts dreaming about a cowboy groom after opening an heirloom hope chest. And rounding out the month is *Montana Daddy,* a reunion romance and secret baby story by Charlotte Maclay.

Enjoy this month's offerings as Harlequin American Romance continues to celebrate its yearlong twentieth anniversary.

Melissa Jeglinski
Associate Senior Editor
Harlequin American Romance

FRISCO JOE'S FIANCÉE
Tina Leonard

TORONTO • NEW YORK • LONDON
AMSTERDAM • PARIS • SYDNEY • HAMBURG
STOCKHOLM • ATHENS • TOKYO • MILAN • MADRID
PRAGUE • WARSAW • BUDAPEST • AUCKLAND

Many thanks to the readers who keep me laughing, keep me enlightened,
keep me writing. I can never thank you enough for what you give to me.
In this book I would like to extend a special thank-you to the following
wonderful people: Latesha Ballard, Katie Jenkins, Candy Gorcsi,
Barbara Goodell, Ken Lester, Marina Tatum, Gill Hopkins, Crystal Partin,
Rita Rondeau, Diana Tidlund, Cryna Palmiere, Beth Woodfin,
Chere K. Gruver, Melissa Lawson and Georgia Haynes.

As always, thanks to the wonderful editors at Harlequin.
And big kisses to Lisa and Dean from the proudest Mumzie on the planet.

ISBN 0-373-16977-9

FRISCO JOE'S FIANCÉE

Copyright © 2003 by Tina Leonard.

This edition published by arrangement with Harlequin Books S.A.

Visit us at www.eHarlequin.com

Printed in U.S.A.

ABOUT THE AUTHOR

Tina Leonard loves to laugh, which is one of the many reasons she loves writing Harlequin American Romance books. In another lifetime Tina thought she would be single and an East Coast fashion buyer forever. The unexpected happened when Tina met Tim again after many years—she hadn't seen him since they'd attended school together from first through eighth grade. They married, and now Tina keeps a close eye on her school-age children's friends! Lisa and Dean keep their mother busy with soccer, gymnastics and horseback riding. They are proud of their mom's "kissy books" and eagerly help her any way they can. Tina hopes that readers will enjoy the love of family she writes about in her books. Recently a reviewer wrote, "Leonard has a wonderful sense of the ridiculous," which Tina loved so much she wants it for her epitaph. Right now, however, she's focusing on her wonderful life and writing a lot more romance!

Books by Tina Leonard

†Cowboys by the Dozen

Dear Reader,

It has long been my dream to have my own miniseries. With COWBOYS BY THE DOZEN, a family of untamed cowboy brothers jumped to life right before my eyes. Now, more than ever, family and continuity feel right, so watching these rascals struggle to grow up, saddle up and marry up has been a wonderful journey.

When I go to the movies, I always search for one with a family element, and if it's funny and sentimental, all the better! Nuclear families, single parents, grandparents in charge—all of these variations on family and the sharing of good times and, yes, even growing pains—warm my heart. Over the years I've wanted to be part of Bill Cosby's Huxtable family, the cartoon Proud family and the British comedy *As Time Goes By* (an extended family of a new husband, older mom, older daughters and live-in friend). Watching these shows inspires me, as my own family does. My husband and I have made it to the teen years with our children—oh, boy—and we've hit the fourteenth-anniversary mark. We've survived things I never imagined we'd deal with—and laughed about it. My kids proudly claim that we're a "fun, dysfunctional family," but I see they're not shy about bringing their friends around. I write romantic books that I hope have the same fun, dysfunctional love my kids are so proud of—and my readers seem to enjoy. What a dream come true for me!

This time I've got a dozen family stories to share with you— and what better ranch for these cowboys to inhabit than "Malfunction Junction"? I hope you enjoy their stories— and don't forget to write to let me know if you've enjoyed being part of their family!

Love,

Tina Leonard
http://www.tinaleonard.com

Prologue

"You need help," Mimi Cannady told Mason Jefferson as they peered at each other with some distrust. Outside, a storm brewed over Union Junction, Texas, crackling and vicious. "You'll thank me for this later, Mason. I just know it."

He turned his head to stare at the want ad she'd typed on the glowing computer screen. The room was dim, almost dark, as the February night had fallen swiftly, obliterating the cold light of winter. Mimi was right: he did need help at the ranch. Woman help.

His family: the Jefferson brothers of the Jefferson Ranch, better known as Malfunction Junction. Twelve men, each on a mission of survival in a family that loved each other, but like an old piano, had become woefully out of harmony.

Still, he wasn't sure Mimi's unconventional idea was the way to get the help he—or the family—needed. "I don't like it," he said for the tenth time.

"What if the woman we get is…" He searched for a word that wouldn't irritate the woman he'd known ever since their childhoods on neighboring ranches. Mimi was spunky, witty, a veritable handful of laughter and quixotic temperament—always into everything. As the daughter of the town sheriff, she'd made a habit of skirting the law, just for fun. "What if the woman we get is not useful to my situation?"

Mimi's gaze turned from the computer screen to his face, touching every feature, it seemed, in a strangely searching manner. This childhood friend of his had gotten him into trouble more than once—he'd desperately like to know what was behind her blue eyes now. Thunder rumbled, ever closer to Malfunction Junction, the only home Mason and his eleven brothers had ever known.

Eleven wild, almost Grizzly Adams–types.

From Mimi's point of view, Mason was little better than his younger eleven.

I need help.

"The ad goes through the agency, you can always send her back," Mimi said, her tone reassuring. "It's like using a nanny service. If you don't like her, you let the company know. But my friend, Julia Finehurst, who runs the Honey-Do Agency, has made a reputation matching up the right people to the right situations. I'm sure you'll get exactly what you want."

Mimi had told him many things over the years,

and, infrequently, she was right on the money. But *infrequent* was the operative word. He read the overly specific, purposefully careful ad one more time:

Middle-aged man requires live-in housekeeper to cook and clean for family of twelve cowboys on a thousand-acre ranch. Must like ranch living, not be offended by occasional swearing, not be afraid of snakes, large animals, extreme heat, insects, loneliness. Applicant must be forty-five or older, mature, able to cook real well. Best time to interview after nightfall.

"I don't like the part about me being a middle-aged man," he protested. "You've always said thirty-seven was just right for the picking."

Mimi cleared her throat, clearly trying to think of a rebuttal. Mason raised a brow, curious to hear what she came up with.

"No female is going to come all the way out here if she suspects she's going to be man prey. At least no *serious* job applicant," she stressed. "We don't want anyone to misunderstand what kind of position you're looking to fill." For a half second, she examined her fingernails, seeming to consider other points of argument. "Besides, that was my only line in the ad, Mason. You added all the other drawbacks that are sure to run off good women. You practically want her to be a goddess.''

"Maybe you should put in something about law-abiding. I don't want any wild women on the property," he said, eyeing Mimi's long blond tresses. Her hair hung to her waist, hardly ever curled or styled, though occasionally she tortured it into a braid so that she could pull it through the back of a baseball cap.

It was hard to believe she was thirty-two.

It was harder to believe that he was the sole care-taker of younger brothers and a family ranch. There was simply too much to do, and while everyone pitched in with the ranch work, the three houses with four brothers each pitifully lacked a woman's touch to make them homes.

An *older* woman's touch, as Mimi had pointed out. A calming, settling influence.

An older woman, even a motherly figure, was fine with Mason, because none of the Jefferson males had expressed the least desire for a wife—mainly because they were all satisfied to continue sowing their wild oats. A younger woman might prove a distraction to their work, and they had enough of those. Plus, a young woman would want a family eventually, and they had more family than they could handle.

"It's now or never," Mimi said softly as the trees

whipped around the two-story house. "It's going to take Julia some time to find appropriate applicants."

Strong wind cried through the branches, and lightning lit the room, showing Mimi's gaze on him. "Though I've attached a picture of you to this e-mail, it's going to be tough to find a decent woman to want to come out here and live in hard conditions. The cattle sale is in two weeks, and I'm not coming over here to cook and clean up after your crew while you're gone. I've got enough on my hands as it is."

"I wouldn't want you to. You might lead my brothers into avoiding their duties."

The last time Mimi had gotten a harebrained idea, they'd all gone picnicking at the lake. Mimi had brought along some cousins of hers from Idaho, and four of his brothers had proceeded to fistfight over the two girls. Mason had never been so ashamed of his family—a female was no reason to fight! But then Mimi had jumped into the fray, and he'd had to pull her out before she got herself hurt—and she'd slapped him soundly before she realized it was only her good friend rescuing her as a gentleman should. She'd apologized, but on certain days, he was certain his head still rang from the blow she'd landed on him.

His head was ringing now as he stared at her, and he decided maybe it was the storm. "This won't be the first goony thing you've talked me into, Mimi."

"And it may not be the last. But I promise you

this is a guaranteed winner of an idea. You couldn't do any better if you were betting on a champion thoroughbred on race day.'' She smiled at him. ''Press Send, Mason. Help will be on the way before you know it.''

It had fallen to Mason as the eldest to rear the unholy bunch of brothers—and lately the situation was about out of control. Frisco was surly. Fannin was talking crazy about packing up and heading out to find out whatever happened to their dad, Maverick, who'd been gone since Mason had turned eighteen nearly twenty years ago. Laredo had mentioned he was thinking about moving east to ease his wandering feet, while his twin, Tex, was cross-pollinating roses with the contentment of an early settler. Calhoun had been eyeing riding the rodeo circuit. Ranger had briefly mentioned enlisting, while his twin, Archer, had taken to writing poetry to a lady pen pal in Australia. Crockett was painting pictures of nudes—from memory, as best as Mason could tell—and his twin, Navarro, was considering going with Calhoun on the rodeo circuit, which would mean the wild boys wreaking havoc on themselves and every female within eyesight. Bandera hadn't slept in a week and was spouting poetry like Whitman, and Last, well, Last was bugging Mason about when they were going to get some womenfolk and children at the ranch. Lord only knew, with the way Last adored women—and they returned his affection—it was a wonder there wasn't a small city's-worth of children at the ranch already.

Something had to be done. The weight of responsibility bore down on Mason, urging him to stay at the helm and not jump ship the way Maverick had. Mason was the father figure, the decision-maker, the authoritarian.

Only with the woman sitting next to him did he relax from the pressure of his life. She gave him other things to go crazy about, giving him a break from thinking about his family's problems. If he was the captain of the Jefferson ship, she was the storm breaking over his bow, threatening to send him to unknown destinations—and sometimes, her storm seemed safer than the fraternal quicksand under his feet.

He always felt on the edge with Mimi, Mason acknowledged, as he reached out slowly toward the keyboard. Frankly, she scared him just a little, always had. There'd been stitches in his head when he'd fallen from a tree she could climb better than him; there'd been a scolding from his dad when she'd skipped school and he'd gone looking for her. More times than he could count, he'd gone along with the schemes she conjured—and he'd always rued them. Every time, he thought, but like a piper's music calling to him, he could not resist Mimi's sense of fun and lightheartedness. His finger trembling, knowing there'd be hell to pay for listening to her, he hesitantly reached out to touch the send key.

Fierce lightning burst over the house, cracking as if it was striking the old stone chimney. Mimi screamed and grabbed for Mason, flattening his hand against the keyboard. Message Sent flashed briefly on the screen as the computer died and the electricity went out, but Mason didn't notice. It felt so good to have Mimi in his arms—under cover of safe, secure darkness—that he just grinned to himself and held her tight.

Chapter One

Home is what a man feels in his heart
—Maverick Jefferson to his second son, Frisco,
when Frisco had boyhood nightmares that the
ranch might blow away like Dorothy's house
in the Wizard of Oz

"I want you to get your butt over here right now
and fix this problem," Frisco Joe Jefferson said to
his older brother, close to cursing before deciding
the heck with keeping his anger to himself. He had
a crisis on his hands, and Mason could darn well
share the misery. "Damn it, Mason, these women
say you put up an advertisement for a housekeeper.
If you did, then I suggest you come pick one out."

A moment passed as Frisco listened. Furious, he
hung up the phone, turning to stare at his ten
younger brothers, all of whom were close to the window in the kitchen of the main house so they could

spy on the approximately twenty women gathered shivering on the front lawn. The women were all shapes and sizes, all races, all ages. Luggage dotted the frozen grass. Frisco, as eldest during Mason's absence, was supposed to be in command. "Mason said to call Mimi."

"Typical," Bandera said. "What's Mimi supposed to do about it?"

Frisco shook his head. "Unless she can make all those ladies disappear, I'm not sure."

"I'd hate for *all* of them to disappear," Fannin said, his gaze longing. "Most of them are pretty cute."

"And one of them has a baby," Last said. "I'll take that one."

"We're not taking *any* of them," Frisco said with quiet determination. From the window, he could see Shoeshine Johnson's school bus rumbling back to the bus depot after depositing his travelers. "I'm calling Mimi."

The brothers went back to their surreptitious peering through the window while Frisco dialed Mimi Cannady's number.

"Mimi," Frisco said abruptly when she answered, "I need your help."

"Uh-uh," she responded automatically. "No. I told Mason before he left on this two-week business trip that I unequivocally could not be responsible for his responsibilities. It takes up too much time, Frisco. I have my dad to think about.''

What bull-malarkey. Sheriff Cannady was as fit as an untried rodeo rider. So what Mimi had told Mason, then, was best put as ''Wake up, buddy. I'm not just the girl next door. I've got a life of my own, and I'm not content to be treated like a convenience anymore.''

He sighed, unable to blame Mimi. ''Listen, Mimi. I certainly understand how you feel. Mason just seemed to think you might be best able to pick through the housekeepers, in order to choose one he might like. He mentioned you helped him write the advertisement. I've got to admit, the rest of us are in the dark about what you two were thinking.''

''Housekeepers?'' Mimi echoed, clearly dumb-founded, much as Mason had been. Mason had sounded as if he hadn't known what Frisco was talk-ing about—initially.

''I guess they're wanting to be housekeepers,'' he said. ''There's about twenty of them out front. It seems as if they came together.''

''Oh, my stars,'' Mimi breathed. ''Twenty?''

''I'm just estimating. *Did* you send out an ad for a housekeeper? Because I gotta be honest with you, the rest of us don't think we need woman help on the ranch.''

''Woman help,'' Mimi murmured. She fully re-membered writing that ad with Mason. She'd typed

the e-mail address to her friend at the Honey-Do
Agency. But Julia would have called her before
sending out applicants to the ranch, and she would
never have sent twenty. Twenty!

Something was wrong. "I did type an ad for Mason, but we never sent it. That bad storm came, the
one that toppled the old oak tree, and the lights went
out—" She blushed, remembering clutching Mason
and loving the feel of his muscles beneath his crisp
denim shirt, and the smell of him, and the sound of
his heart pounding against her ear.

After that momentary let-down in her facade of
just-friends, Mimi had vowed to stay clear of Mason. One day he just might figure out how she felt
about him, and then, most certainly, she'd lose his
friendship.

Friendship was all she had of him, and she was
going to keep it. "We must have accidentally sent
it out somehow." Dimly she remembered one of
them hitting the keyboard before the electricity went
out, but at the time, she'd blindly grabbed for Mason
and forgotten all about housekeepers and other triv-
ial things. Obviously, one of them had smashed in-
correct letters, and sent the e-mail to the wrong address.

Now they were all sitting square on top of a huge
dilemma. And yet, it would be good for Mason to
see that he needed her...in spite of what he said to

the contrary, his life would be so much better with her in it.

But he'd have to learn that on his own. It was said that one could lead a horse to water but couldn't make him drink. Lord only knew, she'd waited so long on Mason that it felt as if her watering can was nearly dry. "Can't you interview them, Frisco?"

"Seeing as how none of us here think we need a lady at the ranch, I'm not interested in that job," Frisco said.

"I think you could use a housekeeper. The place is never clean. Or tidy."

"Then it's our job to clean our houses better," Frisco said sternly. "When there's as much to be done as a property this size requires, we're not too worried if the dishes stay in the sink an extra day."

"Precisely my point. You could use the help."

"But not the aggravation a woman brings. We have you, Mimi, and that's enough."

Laughter, not unkind, in the background nettled her. "What does that mean?"

"It means when we need something, you're kind enough to help us out."

That was the problem. Mason and all his brothers had the luxury of her jumping whenever they needed something. No wonder Mason saw her as an extension of his family. Not that it was a bad thing to have the Jeffersons looking out for her—it had come in handy over the years.

But it was now or never. The tie that bound them had to be cut on both ends, or she'd always be little Mimi Cannady, almost-sis, tomboy-next-door, for-a-good-gag-call Mimi. Toilet-papering houses, tying cans on goat tails, painting rural mailboxes with smiley faces—they'd done it all.

Together.

"Not this time, Frisco," she said. "I have a lot going on in my own life right now. Thanks for calling."

She hung up the phone and went to check on her father.

"SHE'S NOT COMING," Frisco said, hanging up the phone.

"Mimi is abandoning us in our hour of need?" Last asked, his tone surprised.

"See if we ever go fix her sinks when they back up again," Laredo grumbled.

"She'd be over here in a snap if it were Mason calling for help," Ranger grumbled. "That woman's a jill-in-the-box when it comes to him, popping up like crazy whenever he decides to wind her crank."

"I've never known exactly which one of them was winding whose crank," Navarro commented.

Calhoun laughed. "She's been real prickly ever since you drank too much champagne at the Christmas party two months ago and sang that stupid Mimi-and-Mason, sitting-in-a-Christmas-tree—"

"Shut up," Archer said loudly, the author of the musical ditty.

"Yeah, she has been different since then," Last said. "Maybe if you'd act your age and not your hat size, we wouldn't be struggling with this right now. She'd be over here—"

"No." Frisco shook his head. "No, this is our problem. We can take care of it ourselves."

The brothers glanced at each other, then huddled around the window. It looked like a garden party on the lawn. There were more women than the ranch had ever seen on the property at one time, and considering there were twelve brothers in the family, that was saying a lot.

Frisco cleared his throat and drew himself up tall, realizing that the mantle of family was clearly on his shoulders. He was determined to bear it well. "I'll explain that this is a simple miscommunication problem."

Laredo looked at him. "Do you want us for backup?"

"I think I can handle this. The ladies might be intimidated by all of us." He was somewhat intimidated by all of them—he hadn't expected twenty anxious women to show up today. No doubt there would be some initial disappointment that there was no position available, but he could get money out of the Malfunction Junction Ranch's petty cash to give them for the return bus trip.

"You go, bro," Bandera encouraged. "We'll be cheering you on from in here."

"That's right," Tex agreed.

"Couldn't we keep just one?" Last asked. "Maybe the little blonde over there, holding the baby?"

Frisco peered out, immediately seeing what made Last pick her out of the crowd. "She's not a puppy. We can't just 'keep' her. Anyway, she'd get lonely out here. Even Mimi gets lonely, and she was born in Union Junction." He frowned for a second, thinking that the petite blonde would be more tempting as a date than a housekeeper. In fact, he wasn't certain he'd get any work done at all if he knew she was in his house, cooking his meals, making a home for him.

His mouth began to water at the thought of home-cooked food, prepared by caring hands. A strange humming buzzed in his ears as he watched her press the baby's head against her lips in a sweet kiss. The baby was crying, probably cold from being outside in February's brisk chill, despite the bunting encasing the small body. "What would we do with a baby out here, anyway?" he murmured.

They all looked dumbfounded at that.

Fannin shook his head. "Definite drawback. I guess."

"Maybe we could have them in for a cup of cocoa

before we take them to the station," Last suggested, his tone hopeful.

"No!" Frisco knew exactly where his youngest brother was heading with that idea. Once the ladies were in the house, maybe Frisco would soften his stance.... Last had a sensitive heart where other people were concerned. He had reason to be a bit delicate—too young to really remember when their mother, Mercy, had died; too old not to question why their father, Maverick, had left them for parts unknown. He would sympathize with a single mother and her child.

But this was no place for a woman, a baby or soft hearts. "We can't, Last," he said firmly, meeting his brother's eyes. "I'll go tell them."

He went outside, his shoulders squared. "Ladies," he said loudly, "I hate to be the bearer of bad news, but we're not looking for a housekeeper at this time. We'll be happy to pay your return bus fare to wherever you came from."

A middle-aged, not-unattractive woman stepped forward to be the spokeswoman. "How come you placed an ad, then?"

"It was a mistake. We're terribly sorry."

"You're not the man who placed the ad. We saw his picture." She crossed her arms over her chest. "We came all the way to apply with *him*. Where is he?"

"He's gone for the next two weeks," Frisco said,

determined to be patient, not meeting the blonde's gaze, though he realized she was staring up at him as he stood on the wide porch. Trying not to look back at her made his scalp tighten and prickle as if he were sweating all over his head. "We've contacted our brother, and he said the e-mail was sent in error. As I said, we are happy to take you to the bus station in town. Now, if you all will load into the trucks my brothers will be bringing around in a moment, we'll get you started on your way back home."

They didn't like it; grumbling rose among them, but there was nothing he could do about that. A mistake was a mistake, an honest one.

But he'd handled it, and handling twenty women was easier than he thought it'd be, he decided, opening truck doors and helping them into various seats. He didn't see the little blonde and the baby; they weren't among the passengers who jumped into his cab, but he'd be willing to bet Last had eagerly escorted the two of them to his vehicle.

Better him than me.

It was a motley, somewhat sad procession as the brothers drove six trucks to the bus stop, but it was the right thing to do.

They left them in the station, having paid for tickets and making sure they had enough money for snacks. He handed the clump of tickets to the woman he dubbed the spokeswoman, tipped his hat to their silent faces, and feeling guilty as hell, slunk out with his brothers.

"I'm gonna kill Mimi and Mason for this stupid stunt," he muttered to Fannin. "Reckon they planned this?"

"What for?" Fannin glanced at him as they walked through the parking lot.

"I don't know. I just know that when those two get together, there's always hell to pay."

"I know. That's why they can't stay together in one room very long. It's spontaneous combustion."

"I'm going home to have a beer," Frisco said. "And then I'm going to bed."

"No poker tonight?"

"Heck no. I'm all played out." That baby wasn't going to enjoy a long bus ride back to Lonely Hearts Station, he knew. And the little mother had looked so tired.

Damn Mason and Mimi anyway. "See ya," he said to Fannin, surly again. Then he got in his truck and drove home, deciding to skip the beer and go right upstairs.

He'd been up since 4:00 a.m., and a lot had happened. If he went to sleep now, maybe he could forget all the events of the day.

Stripping to his boxers, he left jeans, boots and his shirt on the floor, crawling quickly between the sheets to escape the slight chill in the room.

His bare skin made instant contact with something

small and soft in the bed. ''What the hell?'' he murmured, flipping on the bedside lamp in a hurry.

It was the baby, no longer wearing her white bunting and sound asleep in the middle of his bed, peacefully sucking her tiny fist.

Chapter Two

"Holy smokes, Frisco," Navarro said as Frisco came barreling down the stairs. All ten of his brothers glanced at him. "Your drawers on fire?" Navarro asked.

"There's a baby in my bed!" Frisco shouted. Remembering that a baby could be loud when it was awake, he lowered his voice to an unnerved whisper. "That little blonde put her baby in my bed!"

"Are you sure?" Fannin asked.

Frisco looked at him as if he'd gone mad. "I think I know a baby when I see one!"

"How do you know it's hers?" Fannin said patiently.

"Because she was the only one who had a child that young with her." And the picture of her kissing the baby's head was still fresh in his mind. "I know it's hers."

"Dang." Bandera threw his cards onto the round den table. "I'm certain she didn't know it was your bed, Frisco. No woman would give your surly butt her sweet, fragile angel."

His brothers laughed heartily. The instant fear, which had sent Frisco running down the stairs, began to turn to bad humor. "Where is she?" he demanded of Last.

"How would I know?" the youngest Jefferson shot back. "I thought she was getting in your truck."

"My truck? Oh, no, she definitely was not getting into my truck," Frisco insisted. He would have noticed that for certain. "I told you we couldn't keep her, Last. You go find her, and take her and her baby back. *Now.*"

Last stood up, angry. "I don't know where she is."

Tex sighed. "Maybe she's not here."

"What?" Frisco stared at him. "Why do you say that?"

"I'm just saying maybe we'd better search the three houses and have a look for her," Tex said evenly. "And hope she's not far from her baby."

"I'm not," a woman said quietly, as she stepped into the den from the hallway.

The entire roomful of men rose, half for the sake of good manners and half because she'd startled them.

"I'm sorry to be the cause of so much trouble," she said, her voice soft and gentle, almost shy. "I was changing Emmeline's diaper when everyone left.''

Frisco's mouth had dropped open when she walked into the room, holding a baby bottle. Up close, she was even more adorable. He loved worn blue jeans on a woman; he loved blond hair that hung straight to a woman's chin. He loved sleepy eyes that stared right at him. There was some silent communication going on between them; there was something she was trying to tell him—

Her gaze averted from his, and Ranger coughed. ''You might want to go throw on a pair of jeans, Frisco.''

ANNABELLE TURNBERRY knew what a man looked like without his clothes on, of course, or she wouldn't have two-month-old Emmie. She'd just never seen a man like the one the other men called Frisco—the boxers only hid enough to keep her from being totally mortified.

And fascinated. She almost couldn't stop staring until his brother reminded him he was sans jeans.

This was a household of men, and it seemed to be a normal routine to move about the house wearing whatever. She frowned. Her ex-fiancé had taken his clothes off in the dark the one time he took her to bed; she wasn't sure she knew what he looked like. The fact that she'd just seen more of a stranger

than she'd ever seen of her ex-fiancé wasn't comforting.

Frisco shot up the stairs, muttering an apology. He
looked just as good from the backside, she thought,
taking a fast peek only because...because—

Well, there was no good justification for it. No
excuse. It almost seemed wrong to look at another
man, especially since she'd recently given birth, but
it wasn't as if she'd been looking out of lust, more
out of admiration. After all, if a man who looked
like Adonis took off running suddenly, wouldn't *any*
woman have to look?

She dropped her gaze, thinking that she was in a
houseful of Adonises, and maybe therefore in a pre-
carious position. They didn't know her; she didn't
know them. Maybe she was guilty of breaking and
entering or something else that concerned the law.

"It's okay," one of the men said, standing up to
come over to her. "Next time you see Frisco, he'll
be fully dressed."

"Oh. Well. I'm so sorry for the—"

"Don't worry about it."

The man smiled at her, his gaze full of compas-
sion. Annabelle was relieved because she hadn't
known what to say first, or even what she was going
to say. There were so many things to apologize for!

"You're tired. Why don't you go lie upstairs with

your baby until we can get you back to…where was it, again?''

"The Lonely Hearts Salon in Lonely Hearts Station, Texas.'' She swallowed. "My name is Annabelle Turnberry.''

The kind man slapped his forehead. "We have manners, we really do. I'm Last Jefferson.''

He put out his hand to her, and she took it, noticing that his grip was gentle.

"These are my brothers, going from the top to the bottom, not counting Mason, who isn't here.'' They stood when he pointed to each one, as he recited, "Frisco's upstairs, Fannin, Laredo, Tex, Calhoun, Ranger, Archer, Crockett, Navarro, Bandera, and me.''

"Last,'' she repeated.

"But never least.''

His smile was devilish, inviting her to join in the harmless repartee. She could easily see that he never allowed himself to be outdone by his older brothers. "I'll remember that. Last but not least.''

He smiled. "Good girl. Go upstairs and get some rest.''

"No. I don't think so,'' Frisco said, his voice deep as he came down the stairs. He tucked a denim shirt into jeans, he was barefoot, and Annabelle thought he might be the most handsome man she'd ever seen. But he was obviously a bad-humored rascal, and falling for that kind of man was what had landed her in her current predicament.

Or had given her a baby, anyway. Her predicament of being at the ranch with eleven men was her own fault, a direct result of deciding it was time to take charge of her life, stand on her own two feet. Move away from all things familiar and start over.

My life is more out of control than ever.

"She can't make a bus now, Frisco," Last said, his tone reasonable.

"And she can't stay here."

Annabelle stared at the tall cowboy, her misgivings growing. As far as he was concerned, she was an imposition, which, to be fair, she was, but it wasn't all her fault. It was his brother who'd put the ad out over the Internet. She'd just thought to apply for a job where her baby would grow up safe. And in a real house, not a room over the beauty salon. Or at least that's what Delilah had encouraged her to try for. Emmie would be very safe on a ranch with twelve men, the biggest danger probably being teaching her daughter that cows weren't big doggies.

"Why not?" Last demanded, having appointed himself her champion. The other brothers began a protest that started out, "Come on, Frisco, lighten up," but Frisco raised his hand to silence them.

"Because she's a woman, and it wouldn't be appropriate for her to stay with eleven bachelors," he snapped. "Do I have to spell everything out for you lunkheads?"

"Yes. Sometimes," Last said on a sigh. "So now what?"

"It's late. The baby's asleep. I hate to wake her now just to put her in a truck to get hauled off," the blonde said. Frisco put his hands in his pockets and looked at her.

The dilemma was painful for all. Annabelle realized she was more of a problem than she'd thought. She couldn't match his nearly-black-eyed stare and glanced at the baby bottle in her hand.

A knock at the front door made everybody turn.

"We expectin' anybody?" Fannin asked, going to the door.

"Nope," Frisco replied.

But the door burst open before Fannin could open it, a woman making herself at home as if she always did. "Girl in the house. Everybody decent? Or at least got clothes on?" she called out.

No one yelled back the standard We-got-clothes-on-but-we're-not-decent line. The newcomer latched a curious gaze on Annabelle.

The room fell silent.

"Two girls in the house, maybe?" Annabelle said. "Decent and fully clothed?" She'd wanted to be light and airy to make a situation that was turning increasingly uncomfortable more easy for all. But by the look on the woman's face, maybe not.

"Mimi, this is Annabelle Turnberry. Annabelle, Mimi Cannady, our next-door neighbor," he said.

"How do you do?" Mimi asked politely.

"Fine, thank you."

"Annabelle's applying to be our new housekeeper," Last said cheerfully.

"Housekeeper?" Mimi's gaze turned worried. "She can't."

"Why not?" Annabelle knew she wasn't in the running for the job—if there was one, Frisco had made it clear she wasn't under consideration. But maybe Mimi could explain it better, and then Annabelle wouldn't feel as if she'd simply made another silly mistake in her life by taking off for parts unknown to become a housekeeper.

"You're not forty-five," Mimi said. "That was in the ad, if you recall."

"Forty-five?" Last said. "Why so old?"

"You'd have to ask Mason," Mimi replied, her tone bright. "He was adamant on the age requirement."

Annabelle caught the glance that passed between Mimi and Frisco, Mimi's chin up, Frisco's gaze narrowed suspiciously.

"Well, Mimi, it seems we agree on one thing," he said softly.

"Will wonders never cease?" she shot back, her tone too sweet. Yet somehow strong underneath.

Annabelle's eyebrows raised.

"She'll have to come home with me," Mimi said, with a put-upon sigh. "One of you can drive Annabelle back into town tomorrow."

"Thought you weren't going to help us anymore," Last said helpfully. "We sure don't want to put you out any."

"That's okay," Mimi said, in the voice of a Good Samaritan. "Annabelle will be more comfortable at my house, I feel certain."

From upstairs, Emmie's wail floated down, loud and miserable.

"What's that?" Mimi demanded.

"It's my baby," Annabelle said hurriedly. "She suffers from colic and doesn't sleep well at night. Excuse me."

She ran off up the stairs, almost glad to be away from whatever unspoken conversation was going on downstairs. One thing she was certain of, Frisco didn't want her there—and neither did Mimi.

"NICE OF YOU TO GIVE us a hand, Mimi." Frisco tossed her a wry grin. "We'll think about you listening to sweet baby tears all night."

Mimi was about fit to be tied. She'd nearly not come in time! What if these over-eager Jefferson brothers had hired the attractive little blonde? Mason would be back in two weeks, after all, and the last thing she wanted him to find upon his arrival was a dainty housekeeper.

"I've never seen you jealous before, Mimi," Frisco said lazily. "You sure do put on a good show."

"Shush, Frisco." Mimi rolled her eyes at him. "If you were only half as smart as you think you are, you'd still only be thinking on a third-grade level."

"Mimi and Mason, sittin' in a tree—" one of the brothers started.

She whirled around. "Cut it out, guys, or I leave the lady—and the baby—with you. And *none* of you will get a wink of sleep tonight, I'll bet."

It would be more because of Annabelle than the baby that they might not sleep tonight, but Mimi wasn't going to let any of them know they'd scored with their baiting of her. She knew how to keep this group of bad boys in check.

It was Mason who threw her for a loop. And she wasn't about to have him come home to a ready-made family scenario. She didn't like the fact that her housekeeping scheme had nearly backfired on her.

"We're just yanking your chain, Mimi." Frisco grinned at her, eager to make peace.

"I'll go help Annabelle pack up the baby," she said with a long-suffering sigh.

A loud pounding sounded on the door, and this time, Fannin waited to see if it would burst open again, with someone else making themselves at home.

No one came in, so he got up and jerked the door open.

To Mimi's horror, what looked like a sorority stood on the porch, before silently filing into the den. A middle-aged woman stepped forward.

"Annabelle didn't get on the bus with us," she announced with grave determination. "And we're not leaving without her."

Chapter Three

Desire to get all these women off his property swept over Frisco. "Annabelle and the baby are fine," he said, somewhat annoyed that the spokeswoman seemed to think some type of transgression might be wrought upon his two short-time house guests.

"We have a right to be concerned. We don't know you," she replied.

"Yes, but did all of you have to come back for her? I paid for those bus tickets." Good money, he could have added, but thought better of it.

"Busses aren't running."

Voices murmuring behind her told him that all the women were concurring with her statement. Shock began to spread through his tired brain. "They were running when I left."

"Apparently, there's ice on the roads out of Union Junction. Storm on the way in, too. They shut down the station and canceled all outgoing routes.

Even Shoeshine Johnson's school bus-taxi service was closed.''

"How'd you get here?" Bad luck seemed to swirl around him. If the busses weren't running, he could wind up with a bunch of females—and a colicky baby. The thought was enough to chill his bones. He sent a belligerent glare Mimi's way so that she'd know this was all her fault. And Mason's.

"We hitched a ride with the driver of an eighteen-wheeler who loaded us into the back of his truck. He'd stopped across the highway at the truck stop."

He stared at her, trying to imagine that.

"Twenty minutes in the truck wasn't bad. Any further than that and we'd have had to spend the night in the bus station," she admitted. "That would have been miserable. But Jerry made certain we were comfortable."

Frisco blew out a breath as he looked around at all the women. He wouldn't have wanted them spending the night in a bus station, especially not since they'd come to Union Junction to apply for a job at the ranch. There was some responsibility involved, he admitted to himself, if not chivalry.

"There's plenty of room here," he said begrudgingly. "We have three houses on the property that the twelve of us share. We'll divide you up…" He hesitated at the black look in the spokeswoman's eye. Clearly there'd be no dividing.

"On the other hand, Navarro's house should sleep all of you just fine."

Navarro straightened but wasn't going to disagree with the pointed look Frisco shot him. "I'll go pack."

Three of his brothers went out the door with him, fairly peacefully for four men who'd just given up their home. Frisco was suspicious about the lack of protest. He watched Last shoot a smile toward the ladies and realized he had a bigger problem on his hand.

His brothers saw an advantage to all these women being stuck on the ranch for the night.

He'd have to keep a tight eye on them to make certain there were no shenanigans.

Navarro came back inside, escorting a stranger. "The truck driver was still outside."

"Hey, Delilah, ladies," he said to the spokeswoman and her companions, astonishing Frisco, who hadn't even thought to ask her—or any of them—their names. There were simply too many women, and he'd never remember them all. Nor had he expected to see them again.

Delilah clapped a hand to her forehead. "I forgot all about you, Jerry! I'm so sorry! Come on into the kitchen, and I'll fix you a nice cup of whatever Mr. Jefferson's got on hand."

"Miss, er—Ms. Delilah—" Frisco began.

She gave him a straightforward eyeing that said

she didn't think much of his manners. "It's Ms. Honeycutt."

At this unspoken verbal wall that was suddenly erected, all the ladies seemed to straighten their backs.

"Delilah," Jerry said, taking off his cap, "these men haven't done anything to offend you, have they?"

Frisco shook his head, realizing his brothers had already gained their feet. The females crossed their arms.

"I can take you right back into town. There's bound to be a place where all of you can hole up. I was under the impression that this was where you wanted to be," the stocky white-haired-and-bearded Jerry said.

"We merely wanted to come back and rescue our Annabelle and little Em," Delilah said, her gaze on Frisco. "But we know when we're not wanted."

"Now, wait a minute—" Frisco began, then halted as he wondered why he was bothering to argue. He really didn't want them here. But a look from his brothers hinted that his manners had somehow aggravated a delicate situation. "We were not expecting guests, that's true, but there's plenty of room for the girls here at the ranch."

He was proud of his offer. Jerry gaped at him. "These are not girls, son," he said sternly.

"Haven't you even made proper introductions with these fine ladies?"

Proper introductions before what? Frisco wanted to demand. He'd wanted them gone. What difference did the niceties make?

"This here's Delilah Honeycutt," Jerry said, undertaking the duty of explaining Frisco's lack of manners to him. "And the rest—first names only, since you don't seem too interested, and alphabetical, to make it easy for you—are Beatrice, Carly, Daisy, Dixie, Gretchen, Hannah, Jessica, Julie, Katy, Kiki, Lily, Marnie, Remy, Shasta, Tisha, Velvet, Violet. And you apparently already know Annabelle and baby Emmeline, or we wouldn't be standing here right now."

His expression gave no doubt that he figured Frisco and his brothers were up to something heinous.

"How'd you do that?" Frisco demanded.

"Do what?"

"Memorize all their names so fast?"

Jerry looked at Delilah apologetically. "This may not be the brightest light on the truck, Delilah. You might want to think over your options for the night." He sighed. "I'm a truck driver, son. A good memory helps me when I'm driving transcoastal. And memory games keep me from being bored."

"That boy appears to be the surly one of all these gentlemen," Ms. Honeycutt said. "If you were my boy, you'd approach company with much better deportment. Come on, Jerry,'' Delilah said, with a slight sniff Frisco's way. "It's time you were given a cup of cocoa.''

Frisco's jaw dropped as the tougher-than-cowhooves truck driver docilely followed her into *his* kitchen, some of the ladies following.

"Good going, big bro,'' one of his brothers said, but he didn't pay any attention to the snickers and general laughter. His brain felt short-wired.

For the short term, it appeared that life as he'd known it was going to be very different.

He needed a plan, and some organization. Glancing at Mimi, he saw her trying not to giggle. Well she might laugh, since this was yet another one of her schemes with combustible results.

Vowing not to let it bother him, Frisco realized there was only one thing he could do while he was playing host.

For the first time in his life, he was going to have to be a good sport.

ANNABELLE WAS GLAD her friends had returned, even though Frisco looked very grim about it. Frankly, she'd been afraid when she'd discovered she'd allowed herself to get left behind. Frisco didn't want her here, and she'd been happy for Mimi's invitation—even though she sensed Mimi's invitation wasn't because she was anxious to get her hands on a baby. There was something else going on with Mimi.

Yet as long as Annabelle had all her friends, she'd be fine. They'd been her support ever since Tom had left her.

Her friends were the reason she hadn't hesitated to come out here, at the urging of Delilah and the other ladies of the Lonely Hearts Beauty Salon. Darn Dina at the Never Lonely Cut-n-Gurls Salon anyway.

But no, it was Tom who had left her, and that couldn't be blamed on Dina. Annabelle knew she'd picked the wrong man to fall in love with, if he could be so faithless.

"I'll never let that happen again," she said against Emmeline's soft head. "I always heard three strikes and you're out. I only intend to strike out *once*."

In Fort Worth, Mason had a lot of time to think. One of the things he couldn't stop thinking about was Mimi. She'd been in his thoughts long before he'd told Frisco to call her to solve the minor problem that had cropped up at the ranch.

Mason wondered if he missed Mimi, hellion that she was. He'd as surely miss an ingrown toenail, right?

Fortunately, he had this unwelcome thought while he was sitting in a beer joint, listening to old country tunes on an out-of-whack jukebox. The proper antidote to thinking weird stuff like he was thinking was another beer and a two-step with a cute, obliging regular.

Otherwise, he'd have to start riding rodeo again to knock some sense into himself. He'd been alone way too long if he thought he was missing Mimi Cannady.

Of course, if he wanted to play devil's advocate with himself, there *was* the night of the big storm. Remembering the feel of Mimi as she jumped into his arms made his chest spread with warmth. Shaking his head, he swallowed some more beer.

Mimi would drive him crazy sooner or later.

At least for now, things were under control at the ranch. He'd thank her for that later. And the cattle auction had gone better than he'd hoped. Another week, and he'd be home.

His blood picked up as Mimi's face appeared in his memory. She was laughing at him, the way she always did.

Another beer, another dance, and then surely he'd be tired enough not to think about his nutty little neighbor.

"WE NEED A BATTLE PLAN here," Frisco told his brothers as they conglomerated in the kitchen of the big house. "We gotta get these women out of here tomorrow."

"Sh-h," Laredo said. "They might hear you."

They'd long since said good-night to the ladies and sent them down to the third house on the property—the one farthest from the other two and his brothers. Mimi had gone down to see to the ladies' comfort—except for Annabelle, who was upstairs with Emmeline, sound asleep in *his* bed.

How that particular arrangement had passed Ms. Delilah Honeycutt's military-style sensibilities, he wasn't certain. For a moment, he'd thought she might stay herself, but then she'd apparently decided the other group of women needed her chaperonage more. But she'd given him a severe stare that had said, Don't even think about it. If he'd been hot for Annabelle, the good Ms. Delilah and her icy stare should have cooled him off.

Annabelle and the baby, upstairs in his bed. Sleeping soundly, he hoped. She'd probably pulled off her blue jeans to sleep in...what, exactly? His mouth dried out. He'd never brought a woman home to sleep in his bed. The nice thing about willing women was that they were always willing to take him home to their houses. The upside to this was that he didn't have to shoo anyone out of his house, didn't have any messy reminders of the night before, such as makeup in the bathroom, earrings on the side table or perfume in his sheets.

There was a baby—and a woman—in his sheets now. He couldn't figure what she might be wearing to bed. Something. Maybe nothing. He couldn't identify the sudden surge of emotions he felt at that thought.

"Why?" Last asked. "Why do they have to go? What are they hurting?" The other brothers murmured, as well.

Frisco decided his brothers needed a cold bucket of water upside their heads. But then, they didn't have a pile of diapers and a bottle on their bedside table. "We've got a lot of work to do, and if a storm is coming in, they need to get back to their families. They don't want to stay here for a week until the back roads clear," he said sternly, as much to be sharp with them as to clear his head from the realization that he heard water running upstairs. He held his breath, waiting for the water to shut off, but it didn't.

Water running upstairs meant Annabelle had helped herself to his shower.

She was now definitely naked.

Chills ran all over him. "Don't ask questions," he snapped. "Just help me think how we're going to transport them all back to where they came from!"

"They might be worth keeping," Tex suggested. "Have you ever considered that?"

Frisco shook his head, ignoring the butterflies he suffered at the suggestion. "Out of the question."

Suddenly, the sound of a baby crying drifted to the kitchen. Frisco stiffened.

"Sounds like Emmeline's colic has started back up," Ranger said. "That poor little baby doesn't give her mother much of a break, does she?"

Frisco glanced at the stove clock. Annabelle had been naked for approximately three minutes. *Showering* for approximately three minutes, he amended.

"I'll go see what's going on," he said.

ANNABELLE SIGHED, unable to remember the last time she'd been able to enjoy ten minutes to herself. Em was a wonderful baby and she loved her dearly, but the colic kept her so upset that it was hard to snatch a moment alone.

Even though Tom left me for a Never Lonely Cut-n-Gurl, I've still got Em, she thought.

It was worth it.

The pediatrician had said Em would grow out of her colic—these things just took time. She just needed a lot of love and comforting, and reassurance that she didn't have to suffer alone.

Annabelle completely understood her daughter's needs, because she felt the same way sometimes herself.

Anyway, Tom was, as Delilah called him, a louse. She had a family of women to rely on now, and she had Em. Life was so much better than it had ever been for her.

Turning around for an extra stolen moment of bliss, she let the hot water pour down her back. The truth was, she didn't want Tom back.

He hadn't wanted Em, and she'd never forgive him for that.

Never.

TO FRISCO'S SURPRISE, the baby had managed to worm a piece of blanket over her head as she flailed. "That's easy enough to fix," he said quietly to the infant, with a hurried look at the bathroom door. The shower was still running, so it was safe. Annabelle wouldn't come out in a state of undress he was certain they'd both rather avoid.

He was pretty sure the petite blonde looked good in a towel, though.

"Hey, baby, don't be so upset," he said, reaching out to stroke the tiny back. "You're not alone anymore."

Baby Emmeline—had Annabelle called her Emmie?—seemed to hesitate in her wails, either at the sound of his voice or the human contact. "Hm. I barely know what to do with an angry woman, but maybe it's something a man has to work up to. Starting small might be the way to go." Gingerly he reached to cradle Em in his fingers, and then balanced her in his palms until he was certain he had her positioned properly. Then he lifted her to his chest, cradling her as he hummed.

The crying completely ceased.

"Like falling off a log," he sang to her to the tune of a low country song. "A man never forgets how to make a woman feel good. At least not if he's smart."

She snuffled against him.

"You like my singing, huh? You're the only one who likes it, then. My brothers show no respect for my vocal attributes."

Em didn't object, so he hummed to her and stood, about to leave the room in case Annabelle should put in a towel-clad appearance. "Since you're obviously a lady who likes late-night excitement, let's go watch some Classic Sports Channel. I bet if you learned young enough, you'd love football."

But when he slid into his leather recliner and turned the TV on softly, he realized Em was asleep. "You just wanted to know you're not alone," he murmured. "We all feel like that sometimes, little baby."

LAREDO AND TEX STOOD beside the recliner, staring down at Frisco. The chair was tipped back, his mouth was open, his boots were pointed tips to the ceiling, and there was a baby on his chest. The remote, which would usually lie where the baby was, had fallen to the carpet.

"Are my eyes lying to me?" Laredo whispered.

Tex shook his head, dumbfounded.

"Where's the camera? Get me the camera. I need a picture of this! No one will ever believe that my foul-tempered brother actually let a baby crawl onto his person."

Tex handed him the camera and Laredo squeezed off a shot.

"You wake that baby, and Frisco's gonna chew your head, Laredo."

They both froze for a second as the baby sighed. Neither brother nor infant awoke, however.

Laredo gestured to Tex to follow him back into the kitchen. "I just had a brainstorm."

"I'm wary of storms, myself."

Laredo eyed him wryly. "I'm thinking about all these women."

Tex raised a brow. "You and all the rest of us. Glad to hear you're normal, Laredo."

"I'll ignore that for the moment, in the spirit of brotherhood."

Tex grinned.

"I'm serious here. Give me a listen before you shoot this down, Tex. What if a woman was the way to get Frisco in a better frame of mind?"

Tex gave him his most sober look, which was nearly ruined by the twinkle in his eyes. "Frisco's frame is bent. Totally. I do believe there's not a woman alive who can make him hang on the level."

Laredo sighed, used to his brother's clowning.

"But maybe some womanliness is the way to get Frisco to act like a human being."

"Like a shot of instant female hormones to counteract his overload of testosterone?"

Laredo shook his head. "No, I'm talking flesh-and-blood woman. Like sweet Annabelle."

Tex burst out laughing.

Chapter Four

Tex stopped laughing as he took in Laredo's focused expression. "Frisco has women all the time, or at least he could, if he'd pay them any attention. They practically fall out of the pew in church on Sundays."

Laredo shrugged. "That's pretty much a chain reaction to all of us walking in. When twelve men walk in, I'm sure the testosterone quotient in the room shoots up appreciably. You don't know that it's because of Frisco. He's been so foul lately that I doubt any woman would keep him for long, anyway."

Tex scratched his head. "I thought he was being a pain in the rump on principle."

"I'm suggesting that maybe it's been a *while* since he's had a woman."

Long while was embedded in the way Laredo stressed the time frame. Tex frowned. "I don't think any of these girls are going to sleep with our brother just to get him out of a bad mood. And even if they wanted to, Mother Delilah would freak. She's going to keep her flock safe from us wolves.''

"I don't know that it has to be a sexual thing, exactly. Maybe he needs his own woman to balance him out." Laredo's expression turned thoughtful. "And apparently, we were looking for a house-keeper."

"Are you hinting that we should hire one of these women?" Tex shook his head. "If Mason was here right now and could see Malfunction Junction-turned-Petticoat Junction, he'd be figuring out a way to get rid of them, not keep them."

"But then Mason's got Mimi keeping him all ginned up. How much excitement can a man stand, anyway? So all I'm saying is that having a woman around might make Frisco happy."

"Frisco being ginned up all the time does not sound like a recipe for happiness."

"But this Annabelle girl isn't like Mimi," Laredo pointed out. "She's not the type to keep Frisco in a knot just for fun."

"Annabelle's your choice for a housekeeper? Mimi's going to eat your heart. I distinctly got the impression that the new housekeeper was supposed to be elderly. Not a sweet young thing living here with me, you, Frisco—and Mason."

Laredo rubbed his chin. "It could be dicey," he admitted. "The unknown factor in this is Mason."

Sudden pounding down the stairs alerted the men that Annabelle had discovered her baby was missing. "Quick! Intercept her before she wakes the baby!" Laredo commanded, jumping to his feet.

"She's not a football, damn it!" But Tex shot out of the kitchen, no more anxious to have baby Em awakened than Laredo was.

Their jaws dropped as they realized they were too late. Annabelle stood staring down at the sleeping man cradling her baby. Her expression was one of amazement. Maybe even wonder.

Best yet, Annabelle's hair was wet, she'd thrown her robe on over her towel so it had caught, and the legs that had previously been concealed by jeans and boots were totally exposed. She had wonderful legs and sparkly pink toenail polish on dainty toes.

Laredo and Tex backed up slowly into the kitchen.

"Last had it right," Laredo said, his blood pressure darn near shooting out of his head. "We *gotta* keep her. For Frisco's sake."

Tex swept a hand across his brow as he leaned up against the pantry. "Oh, God, yes. She's too adorable to send back. I don't care how cranky the baby is. We'll all take turns holding her. But to save my brother from himself, I gladly volunteer my services."

"To rock the baby," Laredo said pointedly.

"Just to rock the baby," Tex agreed. "But damn,

if any of those women are hiding such charms under those frumpy country dresses, I get first dibs on the next one we see undressed."

Annabelle peeped around the corner, the robe fully pulled down over the towel now. "What are you guys doing in here?" she asked. "And why does Frisco have my baby?"

Laredo jerked straight. He arranged his face in a Boy Scout expression. "Frisco just *loves* babies, Annabelle. Loves them beyond anything you can imagine. I think he misses having young'uns in the house, if you want to know the truth. And when he heard your little Emmie up there wailing, why, he just raced to comfort her."

She looked at him uncertainly. "That was nice of him."

"Yes, ma'am," Tex said. "And right before he dozed off, he said he hoped you'd help yourself to anything you need in the house." His Adam's apple jumped as he swallowed. "And furthermore, he said not to bother moving Em. He said you're to get the rest you need, and he'll watch her tonight. Since she's so colicky and all."

Annabelle's lips parted, which Laredo thought was an expression Frisco would surely have to appreciate.

"That's awfully nice of him."

She didn't sound certain. Laredo nodded enthusiastically. "Yes. That's what people say about Frisco. He's such a…nice…person."

He held his breath.

"I suppose I'll head back upstairs, if you're sure about this?"

The two brothers nodded quickly.

"Well, all right. Come knock on the door if Frisco changes his mind."

They nodded again. Annabelle left the kitchen, and the brothers high-fived each other.

She poked her head back around the corner, and they stiffened guiltily. "I'll leave the diaper bag in the hall. I doubt Em will sleep much longer, and he can bring her to me when she wakes up."

"Excellent. We'll be sure to see that Frisco gets it," Laredo said. "Don't you worry about Em. She's in good hands."

Annabelle didn't look all that likely to agree, but with a last glance at the man holding her content child, she went back up the stairs.

"Frisco's gonna whup your hide."

"No, he isn't," Laredo said with a grin, "because you're not going to tell him. In the morning, she'll thank him for watching her baby, and he'll puff up with pride and say it was nothing, they'll see each other in a rosy light, and boom! Instant happiness for Frisco."

Tex shook his head. "I don't remember you being so good with relationships, Laredo. Since when did you become the inventor of the mysterious perfect match?''

"I'm not looking for a woman, Tex, so shut up. In fact, never try this on me, because I won't fall for it. But then, I'm a pleasant person in general." He glanced out at his brother. "It's Frisco who's had a problem. Unless I miss my guess, it's well on its way to being fixed."

"You've missed more than your guess before," Tex mumbled as he cracked open a beer.

But Laredo ignored him. "There's just two things that worry me," he murmured.

"Can't imagine that it's just two." Tex sighed. "They must be big, combo worries."

Laredo looked around the corner to check on Frisco and Em. "One," he said thoughtfully, "We're going to have to figure out how we talk Mother Delilah into leaving Annabelle here. She distinctly said she wasn't leaving without her—and there's a reason she's being so over-protective."

"I knew this wasn't going to be easy," Tex said with a sigh. "And, two?"

"Em is only two months old." He came and sat down across the table from his brother. "And that means that somewhere, there's a father who just might show up any time."

Tex swallowed. "Suppose he doesn't?"

Laredo shook his head. "Think of Annabelle in

that towel, and then ask yourself how long you'd stay away.''

''Five minutes, tops.''

''I'd last three. Not that she's my type, but all things being equal, you know, three minutes. I'd want my baby and my woman all to myself.''

''Maybe he's married.''

Laredo shook his head. ''I don't think so. Annabelle doesn't seem the type to fall for a married man, and Mother D didn't strike me as putting up with monkey business.''

''Could be she dumped him, I guess.''

''Or he dumped her.''

They stared at each other.

''That would explain Mother D's protective stance.'' Laredo considered his beer for a moment. ''There is a father involved, but he wouldn't be the first man in history who turned tail and ran at the thought of commitment.''

''Witness the twelve of us.''

''Precisely. Except we'd live up to our responsibilities,'' Laredo said sternly.

''And wear condoms,'' Tex agreed easily. ''Don't get your dander up. I'm just saying none of us have been keen to marry anyone. Possibly, neither was Annabelle's boyfriend. As I mention, this is the problem. No matter how much we might think occupying Frisco with a woman might be just what he needs, the fact is, we don't know anything about this girl. She could be a real disaster. And even if she's not, even if we discovered she was the sweetest thing since southern tea, Frisco might resist her just on principle.''

"He's that ornery." This was something none of the brothers would deny. Not that Frisco had ever been an easy brother to live with, but he had been known to lighten up occasionally. These days, it seemed a pattern was set: Mason rode Frisco, and Frisco rode anyone within earshot.

It made for damn unpleasant living conditions. With it being winter, and them cooped up more than usual, Frisco's mood needed a shot of sweetness.

"Does it really matter who she is or what her problems are?" Laredo mused. "We're not looking for her to be Frisco's dream woman. We would hire her as the housekeeper. Whatever happens after that would have nothing to do with us."

Tex nodded. "Mason apparently thought we needed her."

"Well, someone. Preferably middle-aged, though I'm not sure why he'd feel that way. Annabelle would be much easier on the eyes than Delilah. Not that Delilah's unattractive, but Annabelle's kind of hot."

A cough escaped Tex. "I'd agree with you there."

"Annabelle might get lonely here, but she has the baby to keep her occupied."

"And all of us."

Laredo eyed him. "In a brotherly sort of way."

"Exactly. And the minute she's unhappy, we'll personally take her back to her home."

"Think we can get Frisco to buy it?"

"Hell no," Tex decreed. "That's why you're going to have to go around him on this one."

"Me?" Laredo straightened. "Am I the twin with the brains?"

"I'm the twin with the good ideas. You merely execute them."

"I was born first."

Tex shrugged. "Technically, only because the doctor reached in and grabbed you first. It doesn't give you leverage or bragging rights. You figure out a way to convince Frisco that Annabelle is just what he needs."

"In a manner of speaking."

"Yes. She just might be what we all need, but since that sounds kinky, we'll say she's for Frisco."

"You know," Laredo said slowly, "this isn't a half bad idea. In a way, Annabelle is perfect for us. None of us are interested in settling down. But the ad Mason wrote clearly illustrates his belief that we need a housekeeper, a woman to set things straight around here. You can figure that Annabelle is no more interested in us than we are in her, simply due to the fact that Em is about two months old. That means Annabelle's been through some difficulty recently, and more than likely another man is the last thing she needs!" He sat up, snapping his fingers. "It's a win-win situation!"

"Do you know how few of those there really are?" Tex warned. "Think about it. Every time someone tries to manipulate us into a so-called win-win, it's usually when someone wants something from the Union Junction ranch."

"This time, we're doing the negotiating. Piece of cake." Laredo got up, peering out the kitchen at his brother. "If that baby's father walked out on her, she'll have twelve men to make up for it."

"Probably scare the little angel into permanent colic."

"I don't think so," Laredo murmured. "It's the stomachache Frisco's going to give me that's gonna hurt." He went out into the den to stare down at his brother. Frisco was sleeping like a baby with the baby. "It's just as cute as two vines curling into each other," he murmured.

Behind him, he heard Annabelle's feet on the landing. She came to stand beside him, her light eyebrows raised in question.

"She's fine," Laredo said. "Neither of them have moved."

"I don't understand it," Annabelle said. "Emmie doesn't do that for me."

"Ah, well." Laredo gestured toward his brother. "Frisco has that settling effect on people."

"Really?" Annabelle eyed the sleeping giant. "I would never have guessed."

"Don't let his gruffness fool you. He's had a lot on his mind the past few…months."

"Oh, I see."

Laredo could tell Annabelle didn't see, but she was trying to be sympathetic in spite of herself. He brightened. Sympathy boded well for Frisco. "So, I suppose you were interested in applying for the position of housekeeper?"

She looked at him. "I thought Frisco said you weren't looking for a housekeeper. That it was a mistake."

"Frisco's not looking for one at the main house," Laredo said hurriedly. "We're looking for one at house number two."

"House number two?"

"Four brothers live in one house. We built two to match the original family home. Your friends are all staying in house number three."

"Who stays where?"

Depends on who's got company, he started to say, but bit that back quickly. "Well, in this house, it's Mason, Frisco, me and Tex."

"You're twins, right? I'm having trouble telling you apart."

He could tell this unnerved her. "I'm nicer than Tex," he told her kindly.

"That doesn't help much."

"I'll smile when I look at you, and that'll be your clue, okay?"

She smiled back at him, relaxing a little. "How can you hire me if you live in the main house with Frisco and he said he wasn't looking for a house-keeper?"

He hesitated, his plan stuck. Frisco slumbered on, blissfully unaware of the matchmaking being planned on his behalf. "I don't know," Laredo said honestly. "It was Texas's idea. I'm just supposed to execute it."

Annabelle laughed a little, a quick, quiet sound, as if she wasn't used to being lighthearted. "You're both being sweet, but it's all right. I don't want to cause problems. No more than I have, anyway."

He shook his head. "You're no trouble, Anna-belle."

Her brows raised. "Laredo, can I ask you something? Are you…flirting with me?"

"Oh, yes, ma'am," he said. "But only out of force of habit."

"You're not…"

"No, I'm not. Absolutely not." He gave her his most earnest look. "Neither is Tex. I've got an itch too big to scratch, and Tex is deep into rose-growing and putting down roots. You'd be bored to tears if the smell of manure didn't get you first."

"So you're trying to hire me behind your

brother's back because…'' She waited for him to fill in the blank.

"We could use help at the Union Junction ranch.''

"What kind of help would that be?''

He gestured expansively. "Cooking, for starters. We're kind of tired of our cooking, though some of us have gotten pretty good at it. I'm just about sick of Crock-Pot dinners.''

"Crock-Pot?''

"We throw it on in the morning and forget about it until we get home at night. And it's hot food.''

"Can't complain about hot food.'' She wrinkled her nose at him. "I can't cook.''

His jaw dropped helplessly as his plan suffered a grand crack. "You *can't?*''

"Just pancakes.'' She smiled at his crestfallen expression.

Laredo glanced at Frisco, who had begun a gentle, rhythmic breathing. Frisco didn't like pancakes. "You could learn.…''

"If you think you and your brothers cared to be guinea pigs. It could be rough for a while.''

"It very well might.'' Maybe the Crock-Pot was a miracle invention after all. He could still put food in it in the mornings, and then Annabelle could serve it at night, and Frisco might be fooled.

Doubtful. Laredo didn't have any new recipes. Frisco would recognize his handiwork.

"Do you sew? Clean? Garden?"

"I could try."

Executing this idea was turning out to be harder than he thought it would be. Laredo could almost hear Tex snickering in the kitchen. Annabelle had no selling points for housekeeping. She was pretty, petite, sweet.

She was a woman with a man maybe not too far out of the picture and a colicky baby. Not to mention that she and Frisco hadn't exactly taken to each other like lint on Sunday clothes.

Annabelle looked up at him, her expression kind. "The problem that you're running into, Laredo, is that I didn't come out to Union Junction Ranch to apply for the position of housekeeper with all my heart. Keep my secret?"

Frisco opened one eye to stare at Annabelle balefully. "Then can I have my money for your bus fare refunded?"

Chapter Five

"Frisco!" Laredo and Tex exclaimed sternly, but Frisco only had eyes for the little blonde as she flounced away.

"Well, heck, if she wasn't a sincere job applicant, she shouldn't waste my time. She shouldn't waste the ranch's money," he grumbled, fully aware that he was being churlish. He'd made her mad, and he wished he'd kept his mouth shut. He was going to hear about this from his family for days—and the worst part of it was, he'd sort of been teasing. But with his voice rough from snoozing, it had come out as a complaint.

Annabelle had good reason to be annoyed with him. He was pretty annoyed with himself.

His brothers eyed him belligerently. "Aw, heck," he began, just about the time Annabelle flounced back down the stairs, snapping a crisp hundred-dollar bill at him.

"Bill repaid."

He stared up at her. "Now, there's no reason to be all huffy about it—"

"I'm not huffy."

She tried to give him the money again, but he dodged it, pretending his hands were too full of sleeping Emmie.

"Look, I shouldn't have said it—"

"True, but the fact is, you're right, and I should have already offered to pay my own freight."

Well, he had to admit she was darn appealing when she was in a snit. That was something admirable in a woman, because very few looked appealing when they were fussing. Mimi managed to look somewhere between spitting-cat-outraged and Heather-Locklear-saucy, and he suspected that's what kept Mason on his toes: His brother probably wasn't certain if he was dealing with a hellcat or an erotic dream.

At this moment, Frisco wasn't certain what he was dealing with, either. "Tell you what, you pour juice in the morning, and we'll discuss all this then. I really want to go back to sleep," he lied, because he actually wanted to mull over the way Annabelle looked in the long, silky white robe. Like a madonna, for one thing, and maybe a pinup for another. He liked a woman a little rounder than was fashionable, a bit lush, and she was just right, no doubt thanks to the bundle of joy snuggled on his chest—

"Can you cook *any*thing?" he demanded.

"Only popcorn. Occasionally toast, but it's risky."

He tried to school his face not to show dismay, but it hardly worked. "What good is a housekeeper who doesn't cook?"

Annabelle laid the money on the coffee table in front of him. "I shouldn't think she'd be much good at all." She smiled at him and then the brothers. "Well, since you've got everything under control, I guess I'll go back upstairs. I never knew my baby could sleep so hard. It must be this good country air—"

Frisco held up his hand to halt Annabelle from leaving. "I know this is a rhetorical question, probably, but if you weren't applying for the job, what are you doing here?"

"Is there a rule against bonding with your sisters?" She looked at him with wide eyes.

"Those women are your sisters?" Frisco asked, dismayed.

She sighed. "Really, for a grown man, you are very naive. Sisters, as in emotional sisters. Good friends."

"Sounds like an Oprah-thing to me."

"It is not an Oprah-thing. It's the same thing you and your brothers have, I would assume, a brotherhood. A family," she said stiffly. "Well, that's what those women represent to me."

"They're your family."

"Exactly." Her gaze went to Emmie, lingering with a loving touch. "They may not be blood relatives, but I prefer their company."

"Prefer? As in, rather than your own family?"

She gave him a bland look, indicating that she was through being interrogated. "Unless you want me to take Emmie, I'm going to try to get two hours of sleep."

"No!" Tex said.

"Sleeping babies need their sleep," Laredo added.

Annabelle smiled at them. "You two are sweet. What's wrong with you?" she demanded of Frisco.

"Hey, I've got your baby asleep, don't I?" he asked, wounded.

"Yes, but you're just so…lordly about everything."

"Oh, Frisco's definitely lordly," Laredo agreed. "There are days when we just pray the Lord will get him out of our hair. Not that we want anything to happen to him, you know, just maybe a runaway calf or two for him to chase for a couple of hours, days—"

"C'mon," Tex said, shoving his twin back toward the kitchen. "You must be hungry, 'cause you're gnawing on your foot again."

After his brothers left the room—which was a good thing, because they were getting on Frisco's nerves—he looked at Annabelle. "Of course, you never gave me a straight answer about what you're doing here. And since I'm soothing your baby, I deserve at least a stab at something resembling an answer.''

She reached to turn the ceiling fan lights down a bit, dimming the room. Then she went to sit in front of the fireplace, where a couple of logs were in the process of burning down to shimmering coals.

He sure did admire the way she moved. Graceful, quiet. Feminine.

''It's a long story, Frisco, and I'm not sure which chapter of it you want.''

''Meaning?''

''Meaning that there's my reason for being here, and then there's the Lonely Hearts Beauty Salon's reason for being here en masse.''

''Start with whichever you want to. I've got until your darling wakes up.'' He grinned at her, to show he didn't mind Annabelle, nor Emmeline.

''Well,'' Annabelle said slowly, ''I'm the receptionist at the Lonely Hearts Beauty Salon.''

''And all these women came from that salon?''

''Yes.''

''I imagine the exodus closed down the shop, didn't it?''

She nodded. ''We've had some…tough times in the salon, so Delilah, who owns and runs it, decided she was due a one-week vacation. None of the women with us are married. They may have been married at one time, or had significant others, but there was nothing in their way of enjoying a trip out to the country.''

"This had everything to do with Mason's e-mail.''

"Yes. And his photo was attached. He looked reasonably trustworthy, and some of us are going to need new jobs soon. Delilah decided we could start here on our vacation-slash-opportunity hunt. We're taking buses through all of west Texas checking out small towns.''

"Once you leave here, you mean.''

"Hopefully tomorrow.''

"This is just a fun hiatus, a lark, to see if we'd hire one of you?''

She shrugged. "No. As I said, the shop isn't doing all that well lately. Delilah's going to have to cut back staff. We thought you were looking for help. Your ranch seemed as good a place to start as any.''

Scratching his chin, Frisco said, "I didn't realize there were employment issues. All I knew was that we'd been descended upon by a herd of females.''

"And your standard reaction is to run females off?''

Her brow was quirked at him, kind of sassy. He knew she was teasing him, and he wanted to put her in her place, but he couldn't think how. "Generally we don't respond too well to women coming our way without warning,'' he said dryly. "We prefer to have our visiting hours elsewhere.''

"Mm. Leaving you free to hit and run.'' She looked down at her fingers, which were free of rings. "Well, that seems sensible.''

"We were talking about you,'' Frisco reminded her a bit tersely, since he didn't like her reference at all. He was pretty certain he saw pain on her face, and he didn't want her lumping him in with a possible woman-snaking weasel who "hit and ran.'' "So, you're on vacation…''

"Oh, yes. Well, I didn't really want to come. Delilah and everyone talked me into it. They didn't want me to stay there and…be alone.''

Okay. There *was* a weasel—he was still close to the poultry, near enough to bite, and Delilah was guarding the chicken house.

He looked at Annabelle's smooth blond hair, the way it fell over her shoulders as she stared down at her fingers. It was like gazing at an angel. Even if the angel had a fast tongue on her, she was still a nice girl. His heart shifted as he thought about someone bruising her heart.

This is why I don't get involved with girls like her. They get their feelings hurt so easily when they want promises instead of a good time.

Emmeline shifted, then sighed. Frisco glanced down at the baby. He wanted to know why Annabelle had fallen for someone who'd broken her heart, a loser who didn't care enough to take care of his own child, but he didn't dare. It was none of his business. "And now that you're here? Still wish you hadn't come on vacation?"

She wrinkled her nose at him. "I feel like I'm working."

He looked at her. "What does that mean?"

"That talking to you is kind of hard. You want answers but you don't offer any of your own."

A shrug would have been nice, but he was afraid to joggle Emmie. "Ask anything you want to."

"I don't have any questions. I just thought you might want to offer some conversation. Some minor details about yourself. Like why you say you don't want to have women around, but then pick up a baby the first chance you get."

"She was crying—" he began defensively.

"And I would have gotten her."

"You were in the shower. I wanted you to be able to finish."

"Thank you."

"You're welcome. I didn't know Emmie would fall asleep for me. But once she did, she kind of put a warm spot on my chest and it relaxed me and I dozed off. And now I don't want her awakened because she'll start crying again. What's wrong with that?"

"Nothing. I just wonder why you're working so

hard to be a tough guy when you've got a soft heart.''

Frisco snorted. ''No one says I've got a soft heart.''

''I do.''

She gave him that don't-argue-with-me look, and Frisco rolled his eyes.

''Would you hire me for the job?'' Annabelle asked.

''No. Well, not for my house. If I was hiring, maybe for Fannin's crew.''

''Why?''

''If you needed a job, why not?''

''You said you weren't hiring.''

''That's when I was annoyed.''

''I think you're annoyed now, and yet you'd still hire me for Fannin's house.''

''I didn't say that. I said if. And that's a big if.''

''You're letting me sleep in your room.''

''You made yourself at home!''

''I think you're more softhearted than you care for anyone to know.''

''Well, I'm not an evil weasel. I wouldn't abandon a woman—'' He stopped, catching himself. ''I didn't mean that the way it sounded.''

She drew a deep breath. ''You couldn't mean it in a bad way, Frisco, because there's no way you could guess the truth. Tom left me for a Never Lonely Cut-n-Gurl.''

"A what?"

"A rival beauty salon employee. Across the street from our shop, Delilah's own sister set up shop, determined, I guess, to put her out of business. There's some feud between them that I don't know everything about, but it's pretty all-consuming. For the last three years, everything Delilah has done Marvella somehow manages to do one better."

His jaw dropped. "You're painting an awful picture. Two bossy beauty queen sisters at each other's throats."

She gazed at him steadfastly. "It's really hurt Delilah, both emotionally and financially. She's devastated. And then when Tom walked out on me for Dina, I think it was all Delilah could bear. She treats me like a daughter, and to Delilah, Tom was the one thing Marvella should have kept her mitts off."

"Tom left you for Dina. How did Marvella have anything to do with that?"

"Oh. The Never Lonely girls are pretty good at stealing our customers. We get all the ladies who won't suffer to step foot in a place where they suspect their men are getting more than a close shave. And we get the old men whose wives don't want them getting their bald heads shined by a—"

"Whoa. Stop. Back up." Frisco shook his head. "You're scaring me."

"Don't like haircuts?"

While his hair did hover pretty much along the

back of his neck, straggling inside and outside of his shirt collar depending on the wind and working conditions, Frisco couldn't say he was scared of a pair of scissors. ''I'm a little surprised that a man who was having a pretty baby like Emmie would do business elsewhere, if you'll excuse the bad choice of words.'' He eyed Annabelle and decided for the tenth time that she was lacking just about nothing to make a man happy—at least outwardly. ''And you're not exactly hard on the eyes,'' he said gruffly.

She lowered her gaze. ''Thank you. We've never been quite certain what they're doing over there to steal our clientele, but my ex-fiancé must have liked whatever it was enough to…''

''Desert. Like a petty coward.''

''I don't know. I don't want to be too rough on Tom, because I did fall in love with him. But fatherhood must have spooked him, and I guess he needed a trim and instead of facing me, he went to the Never Lonely—''

''Have you talked to him since Emmie was born?'' he asked, his heart hammering roughly in his chest. What a loser, what a pathetic sidewinder she'd picked to fall in love with! Poor Emmie. Frisco settled into the chair more comfortably, reclining as if he were relaxed, determined to conceal his disgust.

''No. I left a message on his answering machine

that we'd had a daughter. Six pounds, seven ounces, blue eyes, heart-shaped lips, perfect set of lungs." Slowly, she shook her head. "Of course, I never heard from him."

He'd heard some lowdown things, but that took the cake. "Don't think about it," he said roughly. "I shouldn't have asked so many nosy questions. It's not like me."

She cocked her head at him. "I believe you're the caring type. But you play a good game of emotional hide-and-seek. I probably recognize it because I do the same thing."

"What?" He didn't like her thinking she could see inside his head.

"I'm very careful of my feelings, too." She smiled at him, sweet and knowing as if they shared a secret. "I learned that from Tom."

"To hide your feelings?"

"No. He sprayed feelings everywhere like they were pennies easily spent, and then when it came to something meaningful, he had empty pockets." She winked at him. "I think you're just the opposite. Deep, hidden pockets."

He didn't like this little lady looking at him so directly. Her big eyes were taking him in as though she knew him, as if he were some kind of big-hearted man, and her gaze was making a part of his body swell to the point where he was going to need deep pockets to hide what was going on. "Go to bed," he said sternly. "You're getting on my nerves."

"Call me when Emmie wakes."

"I'm sure you'll hear her. She's showing early signs of growing into her mother's big mouth." He closed his eyes to indicate that he wanted to be left alone.

He heard feet on the stairs and breathed a sigh of relief.

Tomorrow couldn't come soon enough. These Lonely Hearts ladies were more trouble than he needed.

Lonely Hearts ladies and Never Lonely girls having catfights in the center of a small-town street. What nonsense.

And yet, Delilah had struck him as a no-nonsense woman. What kind of woman tried to run her own sister out of business? And encouraged her employees to steal customers—and fiancés? Surely Annabelle had been yanking his chain. Family didn't act that way.

Or at least they shouldn't. It had been mighty restless around Union Junction for a while—these ladies with their sad stories just might be the fuse on top of the powder keg the Jefferson brothers had become.

But they would still love each other. They'd never act like Delilah's sister supposedly had. Family stuck together through thick and thin.

He'd brain all his younger brothers if they ever tried any tricks like Marvella's.

And then he chuckled to himself. Delilah. Marvella.

Annabelle had just blown so much smoke into his eyes with a sob-story fairy tale. And like a big dumb slob, he'd fallen for every word. She'd sized him up as a caring guy, and gone for his heart with her baby and her jerk ex-fiancé story. After all, hadn't she gone straight to make herself at home in his bed?

Maybe she knew more about what the Never Lonely girls were peddling than she was letting on.

And he'd just about bitten the bait, hook and all. She'd left the hundred-dollar bill on the table at his feet. It was a lot of money for a woman who supposedly had very little; he didn't know many single mothers who carried around unbroken Ben Franklins. Shoot, he rarely had an unbroken Ben in his own wallet because they were difficult for small stores to change.

The money wasn't necessarily a giveaway, but he wouldn't be the first man in history to fall for a pretty face and good storytelling ability; kings and mortal men alike were known to have feet of clay when it came to such a fatal combination.

He'd been seventeen when Maverick had abandoned the ranch, leaving Mason to care for all of them. As a boy, he'd dreamed of his family being whole.

He was thirty-six now, too old for fairy tales. And too damn old to be deceived by a fiction-spinning female. He shifted the area between his jeans pockets uncomfortably.

Annabelle had nearly gotten to him.

"Close only counts in horse shoes and hand grenades," he whispered to Emmie. "You're a cute little grenade, but I've got your mother all figured out, and you're going home tomorrow."

Delilah would be very nervous if she knew what he'd been thinking about Annabelle. He was guilty, and guilty with her baby lying on his chest, this baby she'd birthed only two months ago. He was pretty certain that made him something of a schmuck. Probably a big schmuck.

Tomorrow, he'd say goodbye to their unexpected company, and then maybe head into town for some willing female fun. If Annabelle Turnberry could make him feel something that might have been lust, then it was way past time to cool down the horsepower in his engines.

SAFE FROM LISTENING EARS, Mimi made a phone call. "Julia, I need to ask you a favor. I sent out an e-mail for housekeeping help, but the help that arrived here isn't exactly what I had in mind. Did you get my e-mail?"

"I haven't had an e-mail from you since the one you sent me two months ago saying you thought

Mason was an unromantic donkey. Wasn't that around Christmas? He gave you a lead rope for your horse because you'd broken yours using it for...I remember. You used it to drag a goat across to Mason's and tied it to the post on the porch to make a point about goats being easy to keep. Of course, the goat chewed through the lead rope and ate the front shrubbery before Mason caught him. Why was it again you were making the point about goats? Or trying to?''

"Never mind that!" Mimi took a deep breath, annoyed to be reminded about her scheme taking an unforeseen turn. Luckily, Mason had been forgiving—she'd even seen a twinkle in his eye when he handed her the chewed-up lead rope. But he'd given her a new one for Christmas, probably to make his point that goats were more trouble than they were worth—and she'd been annoyed that he'd gotten the upper hand on her, again. "I didn't say anything about romance. I just said he was a donkey."

"Ah. I'm putting words where they don't belong."

"Yes, you are. There never was, and never will be, romance between the two of us. Mason is like my overbearing older brother. We rub each other the wrong way. Anyway, I—that is, Mason—wants a housekeeper."

"Why doesn't he call me?"

"Because he doesn't know you, Julia, and we sent

out an e-mail to you about the matter, which he participated in typing, I might add," she tacked on, so that Julia would know this wasn't just a scheme. "Only the e-mail went haywire, and we ended up with eighteen inappropriate candidates, instead, plus their den mother and a baby."

"Oh. Inappropriate," Julia said, clearly trying not to giggle. "Are they beautiful?"

"Some of them," Mimi said begrudgingly. "Don't you have any big, strong women over fifty named Olga that need a great place to work? Mason and I were thinking of grandmotherly candidates for the job."

Julia laughed so hard it sounded as if she might faint from oxygen deprivation. "I fail to see the humor in the situation. Do you laugh at all your clients' needs?" Mimi demanded.

"Just yours, Mimi. And I'm not laughing meanly. I'm laughing at how your brain works."

"I'm only trying to save Mason the trouble, since I got him into this."

"Again."

Mimi sniffed. "He does need a housekeeper."

"And you're afraid he might find a wife, instead."

She straightened. "That thought never occurred to me."

"Uh-huh. Has a...candidate...applied for the post?"

"One. Actually I don't think she's really applied, but I'm afraid that when Mason gets home, he might hire her."

"Since you're not in love with him, what difference does it make? Wouldn't that be a good thing? Poor Mason might like being tied down."

"Not to this girl!" Mimi shook her head. "No, she's all wrong for him. She has a baby, and she's too busy with the baby, and—"

"Mimi. Are you ever going to admit that you just might have a tiny crush on Mason?"

"Absolutely not."

She thought she heard another giggle. "Honestly, Julia, we'd fight too much under the same roof. But that doesn't mean I want someone taking advantage of his loneliness."

"If there's a bunch of women on the ranch, he won't be too lonely. When's he getting back?"

"They won't be here then," Mimi said. "And if you're any good at your job, a very efficient Olga will be."

"A grandmotherly type."

"I think that would be appropriate, under the circumstances, don't you? These men would probably enjoy a bit of mothering."

"You might could stand a bit of it yourself. It might keep you from going off the tracks all the time, Mimi."

"We don't discuss mothers. You know we don't

even say that word when it applies to me." Hers had left her father and her for the bright lights of Hollywood, and as far as she was concerned, all the best to her. A mother was not what she was looking for. "I turned out just fine as a single-parented child."

"Yeah, but it's made you unable to seek emotional attachments."

Mimi gasped. "Attachments are for vacuum cleaners! If I ever met the right man, I'd know it. Now, let's get back to what Mason needs."

"What Mason needs is a swift slap on the head for letting you run his life so inefficiently. But I happen to have the perfect person to suit your— Mason's—needs. When are the eighteen ladies, den mother and baby leaving?"

"As soon as the roads unfreeze," Mimi said, wishing the sun would bring a miraculous fifty-degree day.

"Many people have waited a long time for hell to freeze. It could be a long time before Union Junction unfreezes—and the guests go home."

She didn't even want to think about Mason coming home to find pretty, petite Annabelle and adorable Emmie in his house. Not that she wished them ill—she just didn't wish them for Mason. "Listen, Julia. You send Ulga before Mason returns home. I'll take care of everything else."

"Including thawing the deep freeze?"

"I'll think of something." She eyed her pink-and-white bedroom with the four-poster bed. "I think Emmie would be very soothed by my bedroom. I'm sure my old crib is in the attic, too. Dad never throws anything away."

It was her mom who'd been unable to hang onto anything. No attachments, emotional or otherwise, for her. Mimi was determined to hang onto the one thing she considered hers: Mason. Maybe not hers as in a husband, but definitely hers as in a…as in a…best friend.

"Whatever happened to the goat, Mimi?" Julia asked.

"Oh, I've still got her," she replied, not really paying attention. "Actually, she had a baby not too long ago, a bit out of season but healthy nonetheless. I named it Mason's Folly, because Mason named my original goat Mimi's Dolly. He said I'd been such a tomboy growing up that I never had any dolls, but why would I? The Jefferson brothers would have made a sport of looking up my dolls' dresses." She rolled her eyes; not a whole lot had changed for the Jeffersons. If gossip held true, they managed to get under lots of dresses. "Mason was being a butt when he said that my goat was the closest thing to a doll I'd ever had. He said maybe I could sew it a dress and put ribbons on its horns."

Julia laughed again. "You've spoiled him for other women, I'm sure."

"Speaking of other women, which has nothing to do with the conversation at hand, did I tell you Dad's expecting a lawyer from Dallas to come visit the ranch soon? He says he's about my age and well off and from a good ranching family in East Texas. I can't imagine how a man from a good ranching family becomes a lawyer."

"Dad bailing you out of something?"

Mimi rolled her eyes. "Dad's going to redo some contracts and his will. I'm supposed to show Brian the town, though Union Junction is now iced over in a big way. Maybe he won't make it after all." Mimi looked at her nails, which she realized might need filing after she had mopped all afternoon. "I have to go, Julia. Union Junction's on the verge of disaster, and I want to be wherever Dad needs me to help."

"I'll send Olga as soon as she can make arrangements to be there."

"Great! Mason will be so pleased."

"Sure he will."

Julia hung up, and Mimi switched the phone off with a smile on her face. If she could get rid of the chaos on Mason's ranch before he got home, he wouldn't have reason to say *I told you so. As usual.*

Well, he wouldn't say *as usual,* but she knew he'd think it. After all, the goat incident was fresh in both their memories. In the spring, she'd replant the hedges by Mason's porch, something bright and blooming that would impress him with her gardening expertise. He'd forget all about the goat then.

Unfortunately, numerous females plus a baby would be so much more disastrous than one little ol' lead-rope-chewing, hedge-eating goat.

Mason would *never* let her live it down. And for her birthday, he'd probably give her a book on how to avoid your well-meaning, disaster-prone neighbors.

She touched the lead rope he'd given her, which she kept hanging by her mirror with all the other Christmas presents he'd given her over the years. And corsages from homecoming. Cartoon paper valentines that read You're my best buddy. Joke birthday cards.

All non-sentimental.

That was Mason, though. At least, it was the Mason she knew, and she really didn't want another woman to know him that way. Or any way at all.

Chapter Six

"Sun's up! You should be, too!"

A woman's voice roused Frisco from the comfort of his leather recliner. Emmie had awakened only once last night, but for some reason, she'd let out a little cry, decided she was too sleepy to insist on anything more energetic, and gone back to snoozing.

He kind of liked feeling he had the power to make the little baby content. He really liked her smell, all sleepy-soft baby-powder-and-shampoo.

"Sorry, Frisco," Delilah said, as she closed the front door and began unwinding a scarf from her head. She peeled off a big coat and put her things on the entry-hall table. "Did I wake Emmie?"

"No. She must have worn herself out yesterday from crying. She's been quiet."

"Reckon she's sick?" Delilah came over to touch Emmie's forehead and feel her neck.

"I wouldn't know," Frisco said with some alarm. "I just thought she was as tired as I was."

"She feels fine to me." Delilah looked up at him, her eyes bright with laughter. "I think she likes being around a man. Good thing you had your hands full with Emmie, or I would have had to put my foot down about Annabelle staying here with you. I can tell you're a bit of a charmer."

She winked at him, and Frisco felt himself heat around his neckline.

"I'd offer to take her from you, but I'm about to cook you some breakfast. Unless you'd rather I hold Emmie, instead—"

"She's fine where she is," Frisco said hurriedly.

Delilah laughed. "How do you like your eggs?"

He nearly sighed with anticipation. "Any way you're fixing them."

"I make them with hash browns, whatever meat you've got in the fridge and maybe salsa on the side. How long's it been since you've had huevos rancheros?"

"Too long."

She laughed and went into the kitchen. "All right, sleepyheads, everybody off the table. Good grief, you'd think that was a princess sleeping in a tower upstairs. I can't tell you two apart, so if you don't mind, tell me again which is which."

"Tex." He let out a head-splitting yawn before he could stop himself.

"Laredo, ma'am. I've got the longer hair."

"And better manners," Delilah observed, with a

sly wink for Tex that Frisco caught as he came into the kitchen.

"Emmie is awake," Frisco said, announcing what didn't really need to be mentioned as Emmie's cries filled the kitchen.

"Her breakfast is in the fridge. Warm it up in the microwave for about eight seconds, Laredo."

Laredo shot out of his chair, anxious to do whatever he could to appease the screaming baby. "Shh, sh," Frisco told Emmie, but the red face didn't unscrunch long enough to listen. "Hurry, dammit, Laredo!"

Laredo had his head in the fridge. "I don't see a baby's breakfast."

"It's the bottles on the side door," Delilah instructed. "Just take one out, take off the cap, put in a glass of water to warm—never mind. Watch this. You'll know how to do this next time." She got out a glass, filled it with water part-way, then set it in the microwave for a few seconds. When the timer dinged, she took out the water and dropped the baby bottle into it.

"How's she supposed to drink it like that?" Frisco asked, ready to surrender the aggravated baby. "She wants it now!"

"Patience," Delilah told him. "Are you going to feed her?"

"Not if she's going to be mad like this."

She raised a brow at him. "If you big strong men

think you can handle this baby, either as a pack or individually, I can cook breakfast. If you can't, then I can feed Emmie myself, and breakfast can wait.''

"We've got it under control," the men agreed, Frisco eyeing the eggs that were set out on the counter and the butter already melting in the skillet.

"Excellent." She tested the bottle, then stuck it out toward the brothers. "Which one of you wants to be Emmie's best friend?"

"I'll take her," Annabelle said, walking into the kitchen. "Thanks, everybody."

"Are you feeling better?" Delilah asked.

Frisco looked at Annabelle with surprise. "I didn't know you weren't feeling well."

He really was a handsome man, Annabelle had to admit. She felt much more comfortable around him in her blue jeans and sweater than she had in a bathrobe, non-descript and modest as it was. When he looked at her with those brown eyes, staring out from under dark brows and nearly-black hair, it was enough to make her heart beat a little faster. His expression was intent, as if he truly cared about her well-being. But she was wary enough to recognize how much she needed that sense of someone caring right now.

"I only needed some sleep," she said, taking Emmie from him. "Thank you so much for looking after my daughter. Delilah, you're doing my job."

"Didn't you say you can't cook?" Frisco asked.

"That's right. But I can kick three grown men out of the kitchen and set the table after I feed Emmie." She sat down on the plank bench, making sure she didn't disturb the baby from her bottle.

Delilah turned to the counter, stirring some canned chili. The three men hovered in the doorway, as if uncertain as to how they should react to being evicted from their own kitchen. "It's okay," Annabelle said, looking up. "It's our way of earning our keep."

Frisco drew his brows together. "We don't charge for one night's lodging."

Annabelle smiled at him. "Well, there were nineteen of us, plus Jerry. So we must earn our keep."

"Where *is* Jerry?" Frisco asked, with a quick glance at Delilah.

"He bunked with the other men at house number two. Isn't that how you have the addresses set up? House one, two and three?" Delilah answered.

"Somewhat."

Frisco didn't look certain, and Annabelle decided the Jefferson men had never had need for addresses before the Lonely Hearts women had come along.

That was all right. They'd be gone soon enough.

The front door blew open, then slammed as Jerry came into the hallway, stomping his boots on the entry-hall rug. "Gosh-a-mighty, it's cold out there!"

"Come get a cup of coffee, Jerry," Delilah called. "It's on the entry table."

"Just what a man needs after chopping logs!" He came into the kitchen, offering red, chapped hands to Frisco and the twins to shake.

"Chopping logs?" Frisco asked.

"Yep." He took the towel that Delilah handed him with a wink and a smile of thanks for her thoughtfulness. "Delilah said it looked like that pile of wood out by the fence needed splitting and so I did it."

"You'll be ready for a hearty breakfast," Delilah said with approval. "I'm sure you're starved."

"Starved for whatever you're cooking." He sent a nod Annabelle's way. "No better way to get your blood moving in the morning than chopping logs in twenty-degree weather."

Frisco shot her a funny look. Annabelle wondered why he'd looked so odd. But then, he looked uncomfortable around her a lot. She stroked Emmie's cheek and decided there was nothing she could do about a man who was kind one moment, and burr-tempered the next.

"You didn't have to split those logs," Frisco said, his tone conveying his surprise.

"Gotta earn my keep," Jerry said. "At least that's what Delilah said, and goodness knows, I'm trying hard to impress her."

Delilah blushed clear up her neck, Annabelle noted with a smile. She'd suspected that the beefy truck driver might have had his eye caught by Delilah, but she hadn't imagined the interest might be two-sided. Delilah wouldn't fall for a man who would always be on the road.

Then again, opposites sometimes attracted, as she knew too well from falling for Tom. She'd been thinking hearth and home, and he'd clearly been thinking bed and back door.

"What's the sigh for?" Frisco asked, coming to sit across from her.

"Did I sigh? I didn't mean to." She could barely meet his gaze when he looked at her like that, intense and focused as if her every emotion was of great importance to him.

"You sighed. I know what a sigh sounds like. I just don't know what it means. Are you feeling okay? Delilah mentioned you hadn't been—"

"I'm fine," Annabelle insisted gently. "You have no need to worry about me."

He rubbed the back of his neck as he considered her words. Her stop sign clearly threw him, and he wasn't certain how to proceed. But that was the problem: she wasn't sure how to proceed around him, either. One minute, gentle, the next, prickly— she'd go crazy around a man like that.

She didn't want to think that his concern meant anything more than his sharper moments did.

"You're my guest. I do have to worry about you."

She shook her head at him. "Not much longer. I've called a taxi."

"A taxi!"

"Sh!" She indicated that she didn't want Delilah and Jerry involved in their conversation. Laredo and Tex had left the moment Jerry went over to talk with Delilah by the stove and deftly chop peppers for her.

"Why did you call a taxi?" he demanded in a hushed but urgent tone.

"Because I want to go home, of course."

"I'm not letting you go home in a taxi. I can drive you back myself."

"No need, thanks. They'll have the outgoing roads sanded by now, I'm sure." She shook her head at him, not wanting to feel her heart tremble at his concern for her. "Frisco, you held my baby all night, and I got the best night of sleep I've had in well over three months. I feel rested enough to go home and face my life."

"You mean the chicken-hearted weasel."

"What?"

"Never mind." He looked away, ran a hand through his hair, turned back to gaze at Emmie, then looked Annabelle in the eyes. "What about the vacation with the other women? The hunt for jobs?"

She shrugged. "I'm being selfish. I'm being inconsiderate of Emmie. I thought that going with Delilah and all my friends would be a nice change, but I realized several things during the night." Shyness crept over her, but Frisco was listening intently, so she continued. "I can't run away from my problems. It's not fair to Emmie, when she could be home in her comfy crib."

"She slept on my comfy chest just fine, thank you. Didn't you say that was the first time you've been able to sleep all night? And that she usually cried no matter what you did for her?"

"Yes, but she can't sleep on your comfy chest every night, Frisco." Annabelle lowered her gaze, thinking that comfy chests were hard to come by and Frisco's was a great place for any woman to lie. Steadfastly, she went on with her points. "I can't run away from Tom."

"Does he care where you are?"

"Thank you for pointing that out, but no, he doesn't. My point was that I *am* running away from him, and I can't, because he is Emmie's father, and so she is always going to remind me of him. Leaving town isn't going to solve that."

He took a deep breath. "Are you still in love with him?"

She shook her head. "I got over that a long time ago. But Frisco, it doesn't change the facts of my life."

He drummed his fingers on the table, which fascinated Emmie because she stopped sucking long enough to glance his way before resuming.

"Let me take you back," he said gruffly. "A taxi is going to be expensive as hell."

She smiled. "It's all right. Thanks." Frisco was so handsome, and he seemed determined to look out for her. She'd be blind not to recognize why the Lonely Hearts women had returned for her last night: They knew that she, of all of them, had the most vulnerable heart. They'd been determined that she would not be left in a place where so many temptations roamed. So they'd come back for her.

She really didn't want everyone to have to keep looking out for her. A broken heart didn't make her unaware; in fact, it made her stronger in some ways. "Thanks all the same, Frisco. But I've got to do this on my own."

The front door burst open, and though she'd expected to see more brothers pile in for breakfast, Mimi and what looked to be the county sheriff strolled in.

"Hey, Mimi," Frisco said. "Sheriff Cannady."

"Hi." Mimi barely glanced at Frisco, Annabelle noticed. She indicated the sheriff standing next to her. "Dad says they just closed the roads out of Union Junction on all sides for today. The entire day, at least."

Annabelle sat up straight, her heart pounding.

"What's up, Sheriff?" Frisco went to shake his hand.

The sheriff nodded at Delilah and Jerry. "This

constant deluge washed out the old pipes coming down from the dam. They burst in the night, flooding highways and roads. In fact, they flooded Union Junction square. There's not a store in the town that's dry."

Delilah gasped. "Is anyone hurt?"

"No, but there's a lot of damage. I don't think the feed store or the general store's gonna see their floors for a while. I'm afraid of more ruptures if we have another hard freeze tonight."

Frisco was already shrugging into a jacket. "I'll go into town and see what I can do."

The sheriff nodded. "Be honest with you, Frisco, Mimi told me you had guests at the ranch. I was hoping maybe you could haul the ladies—forgive me, ma'am, for asking this while you're on your vacation, but since you can't leave town, I'm going to beg for your help on this matter—into town so they can help with the clean-up. It's going to take probably two days to sweep out all that damn water."

"I've got plenty of hands to bring with me," Delilah said. "Let me feed this crew right quick, and we'll hop in the trucks."

"No need," Jerry said. "I can haul all the women into town in my rig. That way we can load into the trailer anything you need hauled out, like trash and ruined flooring. And the men can get themselves and their trucks wherever they're most needed."

"I was hoping you'd say that." He shook Jerry's hand gratefully. "Then I'll take the Jefferson brothers out to the dam with me and see if we can lay enough bags and such to keep the water back if it comes up tonight."

"And I can haul bags for them to lay down." Jerry tossed the peppers into the sauté skillet and grabbed plates. "Frisco, call your brothers and let's get this crew fed. Annabelle, call the ladies and make sure they're dressed for extremely chilly weather."

"You can't go, Annabelle," Delilah said, turning from the stove even as she swiftly stirred eggs into the peppers.

"I know. I'll stay here and clean up the kitchen."

"That'll take a couple of hours with just you doing it. I don't want you getting tired out."

"I'll be fine," she told Delilah. "And then I'll make dinner."

Everyone turned to look at her. "I can read a recipe," Annabelle insisted. "Don't look so horrified. Truly. I'm happy to do it."

"I'll pull out something easy," Delilah murmured. "It's a good plan, Annabelle. I'm sure you'll do fine."

Emmie had finished her bottle, so Annabelle put her up on her shoulder to burp as she walked out toward the den. Frisco was piling logs beside the fireplace. "Don't let this fire go out," he told her.

"You and Emmie stay warm." He scribbled a number down on a piece of paper. "This is my cell number. If you need anything, call. I can be here in twenty minutes."

She took the paper, her fingers touching his so that she practically snapped her hand back as if static had sparked between them. "Frisco, you don't have to take care of me."

He looked at her as he shoved wool-lined gloves into his jacket. "I don't have to help take care of the town, either, but I will."

So she was a responsibility, a guest in his home he had to care for as host. "I see. Well, consider me fully cared for."

His lips twisted at her in a wry smile. "You're the most difficult woman to understand I have ever met. Besides Mimi."

She raised her brows. "And I never met a man before who made a study out of being hard-headed."

He filled a thermos with hot coffee from the entry table. "Eleven of my brothers fit that description. I'm the gentle one. If I don't get a check-in call from you in four hours, I'm coming back."

"I'll call you!" she agreed hastily. "Goodness, Frisco. You don't have to worry about me so much!"

"I'm worried about you burning dinner. You may

need instructions for turning on the stove.'' With a mischievous wink, he went out the front door.

''Devil!'' she said under her breath to Emmie.

''But you've gotta admit,'' Delilah said as she refilled the coffee pot, ''he's a handsome one.''

''I don't have to admit that at all.'' And she wouldn't, either. The disaster that had hit Union Junction didn't deter her from her course of action. She might not be able to leave, but she sure wouldn't let her heart get away from her again, either.

She crumpled up the paper with Frisco's number, and then remembered his words. She put it carefully into her pocket.

Four hours. She glanced at the clock, marking the time so that she'd call at the right hour. No way was she giving Frisco any reason to come back to check on her.

Emmie protested a little when Annabelle laid her on the bed, but it was such a sweet sound that she smiled down at her baby.

Tom had never called to check on his newborn daughter, and he'd never called to see if Annabelle was feeling all right during her pregnancy. As soon as she'd told him about the baby, it seemed his heels had caught on fire with his rapid departure.

''He doesn't know how adorable you are,'' she told the baby as she removed the wet diaper. ''He doesn't know how precious.''

But Frisco seemed to know it. And he had no reason to care.

Yet he seemed to.

"Can I get you anything, Annabelle?"

She turned to see Mimi looking around the door. "No, thanks, Mimi. You go ahead and help with the clean-up. I'll hold the fort here."

Mimi blinked at her, then glanced at the baby in Frisco's bed. "If you want to stay at my house to-night, you know you're welcome."

"Oh. Thank you. I may do that." She'd planned on leaving; maybe going to Mimi's house would allow Frisco to stop feeling as if she was his guest, and therefore, his ward.

"I'll leave the back door open in case you find there's something you need for cooking dinner that Mason doesn't have here."

"Is that safe?"

Mimi smiled. "No one messes with the Jefferson brothers. Too many hair-trigger tempers."

"Oh, dear." Annabelle wasn't certain if she was comforted or worried by that piece of information.

"Besides, the ice is going to make it impossible for normal vehicles to travel. It's going to be trucks and sanding equipment on the road today. But if you need anything, you just go out the back door, walk across the stone steps—be careful of the ice—and the steps lead right to my back door."

"Thank you."

She wondered why sadness seemed to flash over Mimi's face, but the blonde recovered, smiling brightly. "Well, I'm off to mop up."

"It's going to be a cold job. I don't envy you."

"And I don't envy you the stacks of dishes in the kitchen. I estimate thirty-four people grabbed something to eat here, including my father, who's never passed up good huevos rancheros in his life." She raised her brows with a teasing smile. "Hope you like washing dishes."

"It's fine. Emmie's going to take a nap, and then I'll get started. Aren't you going to nap, sweetie?" She sat on the bed, rocking the baby as Emmie's eyes began to close.

"What is it like?" Mimi asked softly, her body arrested in the doorway.

"Heavenly." Annabelle smiled at her. "The best thing that ever happened to me. Emmie's all I've got, actually, but she's everything I could ever have dreamed of."

Mimi jerked her head in a nod of recognition. "I would have liked a baby."

She left before Annabelle could reply, but it occurred to her that Mimi was expressing a wish that she didn't seem to think would be fulfilled.

Chapter Seven

"I never did figure out how Annabelle ended up in your bed," Laredo said as he heaved a bag of sand down from the back of Jerry's rig.

Frisco tossed the sandbag onto the dam they were trying to build before looking at his brother. "I think she simply picked the room closest to the hall."

"It wasn't that she had designs on you?" Laredo asked with a grin.

Frisco shrugged, knowing nothing could be further from reality. If anything, Annabelle seemed to avoid him. There was certainly a firm wall there, firmer than this sandbag wall they were laying. "If she has designs on me, it's a design I don't recognize."

"I wish she'd chosen my bedroom to move into."

Frisco gave him a steady eyeing and took an extra minute before accepting the heavy sandbag his brother was trying to hand him. "Why?"

"She's cute. And I like her."

"Don't waste any time thinking about it."

Laredo grinned. "Why? You staking a claim?"

Frisco refused to let Laredo's dig get to him. "She's still talking about Emmie's dad. I don't think either of us has a chance."

"Don't tell me she's still in love with him. Let me guess, he got what he wanted, left her high and dry, but she thinks he's coming back any day now. Once he figures out his little daughter needs him."

"I don't think she's that delusional. Or that she wants him back. I think she's trying to figure out being a new mother and a single parent, though. She's not really thinking about another man. Seems the one she had was enough for a while."

"It's such a shame when bad men mess up women for the rest of us."

Frisco gave him a narrow stare. "I don't remember you being a helluva catch yourself, bro. Weren't you the one blabbering about moving east? Hearing what your name sounded like from the mouths of girls in Tennessee, North Carolina, South Carolina, New York? All those different accents you wanted to study in the flesh?"

Laredo coughed. "I might have been bragging a bit."

"Just a bit. Considering I never thought the girls in all those states would be dumb enough to let you experiment on them. Only way I figured you'd hear their accents was when they said, 'You gotta be kiddin', cowboy.'"

"Anyway, so what about Annabelle? Is it a hands-off kind of thing?"

Frisco quit heaving sandbags altogether to stare up at his brother. "You're serious, aren't you?"

Laredo shrugged. "She's sweet."

Frisco stared at him for a long moment. Then he went back to work. "Knock yourself out."

"I don't want there to be any hard feelings or anything."

He shook his head. "There wouldn't be. I'm not in the market for a woman. A wife doesn't interest me, especially not with the added responsibility of a baby. I've got enough on my hands with the ranch. If I'm lucky, Mason won't saddle me with buying the new cattle in the spring."

"What's up with you and Mason, anyway? The two of you have been at each other all winter."

Frisco declined to reply.

"Is the ranch doing all right?"

"It's doing better than we expected with the last two summers being so hot and beef prices being low. We were lucky corn and wheat prices stayed high enough for us to make a profit."

"So what's the deal with you two? You're always quiet, and he's always annoyed with you."

"He's got a lot of responsibility on him," Frisco said mildly. "I understand that. There are twelve of us, and though everyone's old enough to take care of themselves, he considers himself the father figure and trustee.''

Mason *had* been the father after Maverick left. Taking his place had made Mason more authoritarian. In a way, Frisco was the first-born child, then, ready-made to want everything to go just right. He wanted to make changes, make the ranch better if possible. Mason wanted everything to stay the same, the way they'd always known it, under control.

Frisco wanted to do some things his way. Make his own mark. It made for instant conflict.

''Mason might like it if we all started settling down,'' Laredo pointed out.

''Be my guest. I'll throw rice at your wedding.''

Laredo held back the next sandbag so that Frisco had to look up at him. ''You really aren't interested in her, are you?''

Frisco shook his head.

Laredo sighed, handing him the bag. ''Guess trying to make you jealous won't work.''

''No.''

''I kind of thought Annabelle had a little shine in her eye for you.''

''That was a fleck of baby powder. The last thing Annabelle wants is a man. She's trying to sort out her own life. And the last thing I want is a woman. I have enough fun watching Mimi and Mason try to survive each other. There's enough vicarious pleasure in that battle to put me off marrying for good. I mean, it just shows that no matter how many years you know a woman, you really don't know her.''

Laredo laughed. "Mimi's just Mimi. Different.''

Frisco grunted, going silent as he worked. Once upon a time, he'd wondered if he would ever find the right woman. He turned thirty-six and realized he was too old to be a real father. Just thinking about being a father turned his stomach inside out anyway. His role model was basically Mason, and they argued too much for normal sanity. He loved his brother, but they had two different ways of seeing life. Mason was careful. Frisco wanted to branch out some, test his mettle.

Yet, like the pipes that had burst, everything could change in a matter of seconds. He supposed Mason was right to be careful. There were ten younger brothers to think of, and though none of them were kids, they didn't dare squander the family fortunes on experimentation. In his mind, he knew Mason was probably right, but the caution grated on him. "So, what about going east? You still thinking about it, Laredo?''

"Sure. I want to do something big in my life. I can't really do that with three older brothers. If Mason doesn't clamp me into place, you or Fannin will.''

"Not clamp exactly.''

"Clamp exactly. The Jefferson ship is a pretty tight one."

Tightly run where the business was concerned; wild as wolves where everything else mattered. It was as if they all came together to run the business and fell apart when personal matters rose to the surface. They womanized. They caroused. Sometimes they drank to excess. They'd been known to hold a grudge and sometimes to exact revenge.

"Tight ship maybe, but we are not Texas's most wholesome family. There's plenty of room for you to do whatever you want to do, Laredo."

"I didn't say I needed to sow more wild oats. If I sow any more oats, my field's gonna get harvested." Laredo laughed at Frisco's wry expression. "I said I wanted to do something big, and I don't think I can do that in Union Junction. I figure I'm gonna have to go away to do it."

"Come back a hero?"

"I don't have to be a hero for anyone but myself."

Frisco snorted. "Then what's the point?"

"The point is that I'd know. I would know that I had reached a higher potential."

It was no different from his chafing about expanding the business, Frisco supposed. All the brothers had wandering feet to some extent. His own grouchiness was due to the feeling of being penned-in.

Glancing at his watch, he realized it was nearly time to get the call from Annabelle. He did think Annabelle was cute, though he'd told his brother differently. He just didn't want to think about her too much. Until she left the ranch, he felt responsible for her and Emmie, but after that, life would go back to normal for him.

Pausing as he bent over, he realized she had put a crack in his boredom. He'd been a trifle relieved when the roads had been closed, though he'd been careful not to show that he'd welcome an extra day to get to know her.

That was a heavy admission for his conscience.

"What the hell are you doing, Frisco?"

Laredo was looking at him strangely. Frisco tossed the bag down and stood, glaring.

"I was laying a bag. What the hell did it look like I was doing?"

"I don't want to say, but you being stooped over and stuck like that was kinda weird. It looked like you'd gone into a trance. Is your back going out?"

"Why would my back go out?" Frisco demanded, becoming supremely annoyed.

"Because you're thirty-six. Let's switch. You hand me the bags, and I'll lay them."

"I'm fine! Mind your own business." It wasn't a pain in his back that had hit him; it was the pain of realizing Annabelle was on his mind for the thirtieth time that day, and it was still early.

"I'm getting down. You come up here." Laredo hopped down from the trailer.

"Get your butt back up there! I said I'm *fine*."

"Quit being stubborn. It's time we changed places. You're going to be sore as all heck tomorrow, and we're going to have to keep laying for some time. Don't be pigheaded."

"I'm not. If you don't get back up in that truck, Laredo, I'm going to squash you like a bug."

"I don't think so, since you're the one who can't stand up straight." Laredo did a fake boxing, punch counter-punch in the air. "I could go rings around you, bro."

Frisco could no longer contain his irritation. "I *am* going to squash you, Laredo. You've been needing a good hammering all winter, and I'm—"

Laredo landed a soft punch to his chest, by gosh, it was a baby one, just playful, Frisco knew, even as he felt himself slipping on an ice patch and falling toward the river. A little tap like that shouldn't have thrown him, but the next thing he knew, he was tumbling down the embankment, rolling over rocks and boulders on his way to the rushing water. A sharp pain went through his leg, and the next thing he knew, he was flat on his back and a white-haired, red-cheeked Santa Claus in work clothes was staring into his face.

"You all right?" Santa asked him.

"I'm fine, Santa, sir," Frisco said. "Where's your sleigh?"

"Oh, hell," Santa said.

"You're not supposed to swear. The elves might start using bad language, and then what would Mrs. Claus say?" Frisco said.

"Mrs. Claus…uh, okay, Frisco. Hang on, buddy. My name's Jerry. You remember me, don't you?"

Frisco thought so, but he wasn't sure. There were stars in his head and blinding pain in his leg, and suddenly, he didn't care if Santa cursed anymore or not because he was probably going to let out a good-sized string of dictionary-excluded words himself.

"Frisco! What the hell happened?"

He opened his eyes to see Laredo staring down at him. Now that was a mug he recognized. "Laredo, you dumb-ass. You pushed me down the dam."

"Can you move your arms?"

"Of course." Frisco tried to show him, but he felt awfully weak.

"All right. We'll call Doc Gonzalez. He'll be here in a minute, and you'll be all set up good as new. Don't move, okay, Frisco?"

Frisco wanted to shrug, but he was tired and cold. His phone rang and he remembered Annabelle was supposed to call him to tell him she was all right.

"Guess I should have been the one to call and

tell her I was all right," Frisco said to no one. "She's fine, and I'm not."

"Who do you want to call?" Santa-Jerry asked him.

"No one. She's bad luck. I should have known she was bad luck. Women are, you know."

"Uh, that's right, Frisco. Whatever you say. Did someone get ahold of Doc Gonzalez?"

Why did Laredo sound so worried? He felt someone pull the phone from his pocket.

"Hello?" he heard Laredo say. "Hey, Annabelle. Glad to hear things are fine. Sandwiches if we want them? Well, you know what? We might be coming back to the house in about thirty minutes or so, so if you've got sandwiches and coffee out, that would be great. Frisco's had a little, um, fall. I think he's fine, but unless Doc Gonzalez says he needs to get checked out at the hospital, we may leave him at home with you. Would you mind having two babies to take care of?"

"Shut the hell up, Laredo," Frisco said, his head clearing enough to realize he was the butt of a joke.

"Thanks, Annabelle. We'll see you soon."

The phone was shoved back into his pocket. "I like a woman who does what she's told. She called right on time," Frisco said.

"Oh, boy. Come on, Doc."

"If women did what they were told, this would be a peaceful society," Frisco continued.

"Oh, my Lord. It's going to be Armageddon at the ranch. I hope Doc's got something that'll shut your stupid mouth, Frisco, 'cause you're sure as hell going idiot on me.'' Laredo leaned down to feel his hands. "Are you cold?"

"I've got moving blankets in the back of the truck," Jerry said. "Hang on."

"My leg hurts," Frisco complained.

"We know. Just lie still."

A heap of blankets landed on his chest, and Frisco decided he felt much warmer. Of course, Emmie had felt better, but she wasn't here right now. She was at home, nice and toasty, where she belonged.

"You coulda broke my arm, Laredo. And then how would I hold Emmie?" he wondered.

"Jeez" was all the reply he got. He heard boots stamping, and then the pain in his leg hurt so bad he suddenly went lights-out.

ANNABELLE GASPED WHEN Laredo, Tex and Jerry brought a barely-cursing Frisco inside. "Is he all right?"

"He's fine. Just ornery and unhappy and maybe a bit cold," Laredo told her. "Is it easier to keep an eye on him upstairs or downstairs?"

"The baby sleeps upstairs. Might as well put him up there, too. Maybe Frisco will feel better in his own bed." She watched as the brothers gingerly carried Frisco, mosh-pit style, up the stairs and turned to the left. Gently, they laid him down next to the sleeping Emmie.

"Don't you dare wake that baby, Frisco," Laredo commanded in a soft voice. "No grunts, no groans."

"We're going to need a baby monitor," Tex said, "so that Annabelle doesn't have to run up here every two seconds to take care of Frisco. The baby will give her less trouble than him."

"Shut up," Frisco said, but his voice was weary and Annabelle was pretty certain he was hurting more than he let on.

"It's okay. He'll be fine," she said. "Won't you, Frisco?"

"Annabelle, Annabelle, my country 'tis of thee," he sang. "Shake your groove thing, I'm your boogie man!"

She shot Laredo a questioning glance.

"The doc gave him a shot at his office. I think it went non-stop, direct flight to Frisco's head," Laredo explained.

"Something for the pain," Tex clarified. "The X-ray showed a clean break in his leg, so that was easily addressed. We're not too sure, but he might be a bit scrambled upstairs. He's been behaving a bit oddly."

"Oh?" Annabelle said, worried that maybe Frisco needed more medical attention than he'd got.

"Yeah, he keeps babbling about Emmie. And

you. And burned dinner," Tex explained. "We think that's all pretty extraordinary behavior for our brother."

Tex shot him a warning look. "Not extraordinary that he'd be talking about you and Emmie, of course. Frisco's just not the most talkative man on the planet," Tex clarified, his tone a definite override to Laredo's slip. "Doc Gonzalez would like Frisco to rest tonight and see if he's still addled tomorrow. If he is, we'll take him in for a CT scan. We'd take him now, but the hospital's overrun with outpatient care from the flooding and hypothermia from the cold."

"Actually, we've all been stupid at one time or another," Laredo said with a shrug. "We always come out of it in a few hours."

"Except the time Last got kicked in the head. Remember that? We thought he was going to time travel permanently."

"That dummy. He shouldn't have been at the business end of that bronc like that. I still say Last was just yanking our chains, the freaky little garden gnome. It never takes any of us very long to shake off a little bump or bruise." Laredo rolled his eyes, his expression somewhat haunted, as if he didn't quite believe his own denial of Last's condition.

"How is the sandbagging going?" Annabelle interrupted, all the while keeping an eye on Frisco. He glanced at Emmie sleeping next to him, pulled the blanket closer to her head and seemed satisfied with the adjustment.

"We'll know tonight. We're just going to keep laying sandbags and praying." Tex nodded at his brother. "You gonna be all right with him?"

"We'll be fine," Annabelle assured him. "Grab some sandwiches on your way out."

"Thanks, Annabelle. We don't know what we would have done without you and the other Lonely Hearts ladies. They sure have been a big help in town." Laredo tipped his hat to her. "If he gives you any trouble, smack him."

"He'll be fine." She went to the door and watched them go down the stairs. "Be careful."

The men raised their hands in parting. She went back inside the bedroom just in time to see Frisco scoot the baby nearly up under his arm.

"Come here, soft Emmie, and lower my blood pressure," he crooned.

The baby never batted an eye at the adjustment, but Frisco had Annabelle blinking. She went to the side of the bed to stare down at him. "Do you want another pillow under your leg?"

"I'm fine. Thanks."

"How do you feel?"

"Not as bad as when I got my leg caught in a chute at the rodeo, thanks. I'll live."

"Glad to hear it."

He looked up at her. "Laredo did this to me."

"You look capable of defending yourself."

Frisco snorted. "He took a cheap shot at me."

"Maybe you're just feeling sorry for yourself? Pity-party psychosis brought on by the pain injection?"

"Maybe." He closed his eyes before opening them to look at her steadfastly. "Come here and kiss me, Annabelle."

Chapter Eight

Annabelle's lips parted. Kiss Frisco? No way. Not while he was lying in a bed and medicated to the max. Kiss him? Never. Not while she was trying to get her life together. What a very bad idea.

She decided to ignore him.

"I'm sure a small kiss is all the medication I'd need, Anna-anna-bella-bella. Bella Anna."

Her brows puckered. "Frisco, you obviously don't handle medicine very well. Maybe I'll have the doctor splint your mouth to match your leg."

He squinted at her. "Just a quick one, to make my ouchy go away."

She rolled her eyes at the big man, trussed up, helpless, with a baby under his arm, spouting nonsense. "Pathetic, Frisco. Really. You won't want to remember this conversation in the morning."

"I think you like me. Don't you, Annabelle? Emmie sure does."

"Emmie's designs on you are not the same as

mine,'' she said starchily. Sitting down in the rocker across from him, she pulled out a book. ''I have to wash some things, so go to sleep.''

''I'll only be helpless one day. I want my kiss now, while I'm half-anaesthetized.''

''What good does that do?'' Her heart beat harder as she considered his silly pleading.

''It makes me brave enough to ask a woman I know I shouldn't ask for anything. Under normal circumstances, that is.''

''So you're saying that a quick, sisterly kiss is something we could both forget when the drugs wear off.'' Her brow quirked.

''I don't know. Do drugs work like alcohol?''

''Do you often kiss women while you're alcohol-impaired just so you won't have to remember your behavior?''

''I don't think so. I've always had to be fairly responsible.'' His brow furrowed. ''Maybe that's why I'm so tempted now.''

''Well, I'm not impaired. And I'd remember.'' Likely, she'd never forget it. He was a very appealing man.

He brightened. ''We could get you impaired. Maybe Doc Gonzalez could give you a shot, too.''

''Thanks, no,'' she said hastily. ''I had enough of those in the hospital having Emmie.''

''Oh. Well, then, I guess I'm just going to have to do without.'' His expression turned sad.

"Yes, I think you are."

"Maybe it's better that way."

"I'm sure it is."

"I probably wouldn't like kissing you."

Now he was heading from pathetic to whiny manipulative. Two could play that game. "I *know* I wouldn't like kissing you."

"Betcha a hundred bucks you would," he said confidently.

She laughed. "I don't need a hundred bucks."

He frowned. "I'll bet you your hundred-dollar bill back that you'll like kissing me."

"Really, Frisco, you have nothing to prove, and I don't need the money."

"Why not? Emmie might need a new dress some day."

"I'm financially able to take care of Emmie. Don't worry about her. And I owed you for the bus ticket. Why don't you go to sleep now? You have to be tired."

"Strangely enough, I feel strung like a bad guitar string."

Great. She had to baby-sit the only six-foot-four male who went hyper on pain medication. Heaven forbid he should fold like a tent the way most people would.

"I changed my mind," Frisco said suddenly. "I don't want you to kiss me." The fog had left his mind for just a minute, long enough for him to know he was making a royal ass of himself. She smelled good, like roses in his mother's garden. Blond hair pushed back by a white headband fell smoothly in a gleaming curve to the edge of her chin. China-blue eyes, fringed by long black lashes, regarded him intently, stripping him of his bravado. She had full supple lips which were slicked with some kind of clear gloss, lips which Frisco thought would be fabulous for kissing and soothing other parts of his body, as well.

He stopped those thoughts in a hurry. Miss Annabelle and her dainty dress were a nightmare to a man who should want nothing more than to get her the hell out of his bedroom in a hurry. She was testing the limit of his strength—and worse, she'd made it clear she wanted no part of him. Had he really thought she would?

"I'd like a blanket, please. There's one in the bottom of that dresser." Emmie could probably use a blanket, too. All she had was her baby blanket over her, and he didn't want her catching a chill.

Annabelle got up, walked to the dresser, bent down to open the drawer. The white eyelet dress slid up a good three inches, revealing strong white legs, despite her quick tug at the hem to keep it in place. A sudden nurse fantasy ran all over him, making him hotter than a branding iron in a fire. But this was Annabelle. He couldn't indulge in a nurse fantasy about her!

Closing the drawer, she turned, the cotton blanket in her hands.

Too late.

"Oh, my," she said.

He groaned, unable to hide the erection making a tent of the sheet.

The front door slammed downstairs. Boots sounded on the stairwell.

Annabelle's gaze met Frisco's, then flew to his predicament. In a reflex action that caught him completely off-guard, she flung the folded blanket across the five-foot distance between them.

The heavy cotton landed on his lap with a thud, whooshing the air out of him and flattening whatever pride he had left.

"Annabelle, here's a bottle of painkillers Doc Gonzalez thought Frisco might need," Laredo said, stepping into the room, talking quietly until he saw that Frisco was awake and the baby was still asleep. "Dang, it's hotter than hopping toads on summer cement in here, Frisco. Whaddya need a blanket for? Should I get you a fan?"

"No," Frisco said between clenched teeth, his ears ringing.

"Perhaps he needs a pain pill rather than a blanket," Laredo told Annabelle. "The doc said the shot wouldn't last more than four hours or six, maybe. But Frisco's so darn big, maybe it already wore off."

"We'll give him a while longer. Thanks."

She smiled demurely at Laredo, and he smiled back, clearly taking a second look at the delicate woman. Frisco allowed his head to fall back against the pillow as he closed his eyes. Laredo's boots thumped down the stairs, and the front door slammed.

"You did that on purpose," he complained.

"Should I have left you sticking up? Seemed awkward to me." Annabelle jerked open the bedside drawer to toss the bottle of painkillers inside.

"I would have thought of something. It wasn't necessary for you to...crush me."

"I suppose thanking me for saving you from humiliation would be too much to ask for."

"I'd rather be slightly embarrassed than—"

"Oh, hush. You'd argue with the devil himself." Annabelle glanced in the drawer. "If I give you a pain pill, do you think you'd O.D.? I don't want that on my conscience, but I would love for you to go to sleep. How are you feeling in general?"

"I think the stars have faded from my vision. I'm only seeing black dots now."

"Fine." She started to slam the drawer shut, but something caught her attention.

Frisco's breath caught in his throat. Surely she wouldn't say anything about his stash.

"Is this what the well-dressed man wears nowadays?" She held up a condom in a bright package.

"Striped with fluorescent colors," she read. "And this one says it has stars and an interesting device on the tip for maximum pleasure."

He'd take back the part about preferring humiliation to pain.

"I had no idea these things came in any other style besides plain old, plain old."

"Now you know." He wasn't going to say anything more than that. He wanted her out of his drawer. "Would you quit rummaging around in there?"

She closed the drawer. "Sorry. But a guy who dresses to impress shouldn't be upset if a gal looks at the suits." Rising, she straightened the blanket briskly. "Did you really want this, or did you just need camouflage?"

"I'll keep the camouflage."

"I think that's best." She settled into the rocker across the room. "Go to sleep. Please."

"You sit there and be quiet, and maybe I can."

Shrugging, she opened a book, placing it in her lap as she curled up in the rocker. The dress slid to her knees and Frisco closed his eyes, shutting out the alluring picture she made.

If Laredo had ever wanted to punish Frisco for anything he'd ever done to his younger brother, he'd picked an excellent method.

Torture.

ANNABELLE RECOGNIZED at once that taking care of a newborn was a piece of cake compared to a male who was used to independence and overriding everything in his path.

Gently, she moved Emmie to a pallet on the floor, covertly studying the big man who was just as studiously ignoring her. His eyes were closed so she couldn't see the dark-brown irises. Ebony brows complemented black hair which lay unruly against the pillow. He still had an obvious dilemma, which fascinated Annabelle. Surely it should have deflated by now? She thought about Tom and frowned. His hadn't lasted so long. Nor had it been so...

"What are you reading?"

She started a little at the brusque question and hoped he hadn't seen her staring at the blanket. "A romance."

"Isn't that a little racy for a new mom?"

"Happy endings are good for me."

He was silent, looking at her with those dark eyes. Annabelle went back to staring at a page. She did feel a bit isolated now that she was a single mother. Her relationship with Tom had left her wondering if there was any kindling left to start a fire with if she ever met a man she might like. Tom had sucked a lot of the heat from her life.

She certainly hadn't felt with Tom the way she did right now. Frisco's laser-like focus on her made her feel as if she might burst into flames any second.

It was best to quit pretending he didn't affect her—she was pretty sure he'd figure out her secret soon if she wasn't careful.

"Since you're not going to fall asleep, I'm going to go downstairs and do some things. Call me if you need me."

He was silent.

"Frisco, I'm just not interested in testing the water with anyone."

"I know. I'm not, either." He shook his head. "I don't know why I wanted to kiss you. I'm sorry."

"I was tempted, you know." It wasn't necessary to beat his ego to smithereens.

"If that was tempted, you made Eve look bad."

She smiled at him. "If things were different, if I didn't have a newborn, I might be up for a quick kiss with a man I barely know."

"I lost my mind for a minute, Annabelle. It won't happen again. I sure didn't mean to make you uncomfortable."

She smiled slightly. "Your leg's broken. It levels the playing field quite a bit. I can resist from five feet away."

"I wouldn't want you unless you wanted me."

"Okay."

"Do you?"

She laughed. "No," she told him, aware that the hopeful expression on his face was due to the painkillers scrambling his brain. Frisco and drugs were not a successful mix.

"Damn."

"I could get Laredo to find you another nurse. There're other Lonely Hearts ladies here."

"No, thanks," he said hurriedly. "I like you. But not in *that way,* of course."

"Of course. Go to sleep."

She left the room, her heart practically pounding in her ears. Too much man, too much temptation for her damaged ego to resist. Tom had never wanted her that way. Being the focus of Frisco's intoxicated interest was way more flattering—and sensual—than anything she'd ever known.

It would be so nice to give in. He probably wouldn't have remembered it tomorrow. Just a kiss. What would it have hurt?

Everything, of course. Because sometimes kissing was the start of something bigger.

And that was a risk she simply couldn't take.

Chapter Nine

"So run this thing about the big-haired beauty queens across the street by me one more time. The…what'd you call them? The Snip-n-Snarls? Brush-n-Babes?"

Frisco's voice in the dark startled Annabelle. She'd come in to sneak Emmie out of Frisco's room. "I'm skipping storytime right now, Frisco. Go back to sleep."

"I just want to know what makes your customers desert Ms. Delilah."

Annabelle reached inside the bathroom and flipped on the light before closing the door. Just a crack of illumination shone into the dark bedroom. "We've long wondered ourselves. Delilah and her stylists are very good with hair, and the customers seem satisfied—until they find out about the shop across the street. One try over there, and the men never come back to us." Including Tom, but that fact was redundant, no need to mention it again.

"They attend church with nicks out of their hair, though, and it's easy to tell where they were Saturday night. It's almost like a visual roll call." She lowered her voice. "To be honest, I'm not certain all those Cut-n-Gurls have beauty-school training. Delilah says she doesn't know when Marvella would have gone to school." She shrugged. "Of course, there's not so much to cutting a man's hair, I suppose. Their tool of choice appears to be clippers. You'll notice the men who frequent their salon tend to sport short, uneven silhouettes, which has always reminded me of a golf course with divots missing here and there."

"There has to be something you're not telling me. And since I can't sleep, I'm in the mood for a story."

She was pretty tired. The men and women had all returned from sandbagging, sweeping out water, and whatever other duties they'd been assigned. She'd cooked dinner, had it hot and ready—a recipe from an old file she'd found in the kitchen—and fed what seemed like an army of people. Chicken soup, a monster-sized bowl of green salad, and King Ranch casserole. She'd given herself an A for Edibility, but it had meant a lot of clean-up time in the kitchen. Everyone was gone now, except for Laredo and Tex, who'd showered and gone to bed in their own rooms. Right now, she could fall asleep on the floor.

"I can't tell you a story because I have to get

some sleep. But I'll give you a bit of gossip I've mulled many times since I heard it. Supposedly— and this is just gossip, I certainly don't know for sure—on the wall of their salon is written in big, sparkly gold letters: Save a horse, ride a cowboy.''

"I can see where that might be appealing.''

"Frisco!''

He chuckled. "I've been needing a haircut for a while now—''

"Frisco, I think I'd consider that desertion at the minimum and disregarding my confidences at the maximum. Now I'm going to bed.'' He wasn't supposed to have been amused, and he darn sure wasn't supposed to be interested!

"Come on. I was only playing.''

"Playing dumb?'' How could he joke after what she'd told him about Tom?

"Trying to keep you in here a while longer.''

"Not like that, you aren't. Friends understand where the line shouldn't be crossed.''

"I guess I didn't realize we were friends, Annabelle. I'm happy to hear you say that.''

"I have to help you to the bathroom, don't I? Surely assisting you makes us more than acquaintances.''

"You're real antsy about that salon, aren't you?''

She rolled her eyes in the dark. "To say the least, especially for Delilah's sake. Anyway, how do you think you'd feel, if someone made a joke about someone you'd once cared about?''

He thought about Laredo teasing him about Annabelle. ''I'd probably want to squish his head.''

''Lie real still so I can use your brand of revenge on you.''

''I wouldn't really be interested in a woman who compared riding me to riding a horse.''

Her brows shot up; she could feel her face pink. She and Tom had made love once. It had been nothing like riding a horse. In fact, it had been more like...riding her first bike. One second she'd been on; the next second she'd tumbled to the ground.

''Annabelle, have you noticed how much this baby's been sleeping?''

His soft voice shifted her away from her disheartening thoughts. ''She's obviously joining you in your lazy habits.''

''Hmm. Maybe she's decided to give me a second chance.''

''To do what?'' Ever since Frisco had held Emmie, she'd been charmed into sleeping better.

''To get to know her.''

''Frisco, my daughter is innocent. I no longer am. And I really don't want to get to know you, if that's what you're implying. You're a big, ornery male. I want peace and quiet in my life. I will never get that with you.''

''No, you won't. I readily admit that.''

They were both quiet for a moment. Then he said, "Might as well lie down on the opposite side of the bed, Annabelle. There's plenty of room. I promise not to even breathe on you."

She was so tired. The alternative was finding another bed somewhere in the house, and frankly, she didn't want to root through bedrooms in case she opened a door where one of the other brothers was sleeping. She wasn't even certain there was another bedroom.

"I snore," she told him.

"That will be annoying. I'll toss this blanket over your head. The one you used on me."

She giggled and edged cautiously to the side of the bed. "You should have seen your face."

"You should have seen yours. You looked like you'd never seen a man in that condition before."

Her smile melted away. She hadn't—at least not like Frisco. But she wasn't going to tell this irritating cowboy that. He was cocky and conceited, and she'd be embarrassed. Besides, that was all more private than she cared to share. "Shut up, Frisco," she said, instead. "If I'm sleeping in here with you for the sake of convenience, you have to be quiet. You're going to wake Emmie."

"She's used to my voice by now. She doesn't even stir until she wants a bottle or a diaper change."

Annabelle sighed to herself and slid into bed with

her dress on, but decided that was uncomfortable. The little bit of light was necessary, but it left her having to sleep with her eyelet dress on. Dare she slip it off and doze in her underthings?

No. "Is the light bothering you?" she asked.

"I'd rather it be dark, but I didn't want to suggest it. You're awfully tense about us sharing a bed."

"I'm tense about you in general," she said, getting up to flip off the light. "Goodness knows, I can't imagine why I feel that way."

"I can't, either," he agreed, way too cheerfully for her liking.

"Good *night,* Frisco," she stressed so he'd cease his teasing.

"Good night, Annabelle."

She sighed as she hit the pillow. For a moment, she wondered if she would really be able to sleep in the same bed with Frisco, but in a way, she felt oddly comforted with him in the same room.

Even in the same bed.

"Dinner was good, Annabelle," he said, sounding sleepy.

"Thank you." She felt warmed by his praise. Okay, maybe he wasn't all that bad. Cranky, sure. The truth was, she didn't know what kind of man she could trust anymore. Tom had been all blond hair and blue eyes come-on, and she'd desperately needed that at the time. Her world had turned dark after her father died, and there was Tom, light and airy and interested. She had fallen like a sack of potatoes from a truck.

It would be textbook cliché now to turn around and fall for Tom's total opposite. If she'd figured nothing else out about herself, it was that she was still grieving, still running—and sooner or later, a girl had to slow down.

"Annabelle?" Frisco said.

"Yes?"

"You sure are the prettiest housekeeper we've ever had."

"I wasn't aware you'd had any before."

"I want you to focus on the compliment and not the comment."

Her eyes snapped open in the dark. A shiver ran over her. Was he making a pass at her? Surely not. Certainly he seemed to like Emmie, but more often than not, he seemed out of sorts around Annabelle. "Um, thank you," she murmured uncertainly.

"Annabelle?"

"Yes?"

"I've been wanting to kiss you ever since I first laid eyes on you. I wouldn't, of course. But I did think about it."

Her breath caught for an instant. And then she dove in wearing only courage. "I've thought about kissing you, too," she whispered. She squeezed her eyes tightly shut.

To her surprise, Frisco rolled over to face her. She

couldn't see him, but she knew he was close to her face. He smelled good, and his nearness touched her skin with warmth. Instantly, she wanted to get closer to him, pull him to her.

When he brushed her hair away from her face, she sighed with longing.

"I shouldn't, Annabelle," he murmured. "It would be ungentlemanly to take advantage of you."

She thought she'd already had a man take advantage of her—and it hadn't felt like this. Just Frisco's voice made her shiver inside. She wanted him to touch her.

And then he did, with his lips. First, brushing against her forehead, and then along her cheeks. Then her eyelids. Annabelle's insides seemed to contract, as if her inner soul knew exactly what it wanted from him. In spite of his size and his gruff exterior, Frisco was soft and gentle and not scary at all.

His lips touched hers suddenly, and Annabelle realized he'd been going slowly with her, gentling her. His patience made her relax so that she melted against him.

Frisco felt Annabelle give into him. It was a surrender.

He hadn't expected it. She was so delicate and ethereal, like mythical magical moonflies beating their wings at night. He wanted desperately to catch her, to hold her, to rub her magic all over him.

Caught off-guard, his whole body afire, Frisco forced himself to pull away.

"Good night, Annabelle," he said hoarsely.

IN THE NIGHT, the sandbags held back the water. Though the temperature struggled up above the freezing mark, the ice stayed on the roads.

"I'm hauling the ladies into town. They're going to do some mopping and other things," Jerry told Annabelle. "Will you be all right here? Or do you and Emmie want to come with us?"

Emmie was behaving so much better that, as much as Annabelle would have loved to leave, she decided it was better for her baby to stay put. Frisco had a wonderfully comforting touch for Emmie's colic. Helping out here was a small price for Emmie's welfare. But just for tonight. "I'll stay and cook. Jerry, when are you heading back?"

"Good Lord willing and the creek doesn't rise, tomorrow, little lady. Why do you ask?"

She looked into his cheery blue eyes. "I need to get going myself."

"Ah. Cabin fever?"

"Something like that."

"Frisco fever?"

"Close enough to be right on the mark." She sighed. "I'm just ready to move on."

"Delilah says you'd been 'moving on' for a couple months before you came into her shop. That she hired you right off the street because you looked tired and haunted. Something eating you, Annabelle?'' He gave her a kindly smile, his cheeks rosy from cold. ''I got real big shoulders to cry on.''

''No. No, thanks,'' she said hurriedly. ''I'm fine. I just need to get back.''

''To the salon? I don't know yet that the ladies are going back tomorrow. They may head farther east. They're still on vacation, you know.''

''I'm not going back to the salon. Don't tell Delilah, Jerry. I want to tell her myself, please.''

''Fair enough. We roll at 8:00 a.m. Can you and Emmie be ready?''

''We'll be ready, Jerry. Thanks.''

He touched his cap and walked across the yard toward his truck. She headed into the kitchen, hurrying upstairs to retrieve Emmie before the baby began a full-scale assault for her bottle.

Frisco lay on the bed, sound asleep, his leg awkwardly propped up, his body turned uncomfortably. He was beautiful when he slept, dark and masterful. Emmie, unaware that she was sleeping next to a giant, had scooched up under his arm, her diapered rump in the air, her fist in her mouth.

Annabelle wished she had a camera. She'd like to remember Emmie having this moment with a man, nearly a father-figure. Maybe the only man who would ever nap with her like that. Her eyes clouded. Maybe I've just made a total wreck of my life and

Emmie's, she thought. The last thing I ever meant to do was hurt her.

The blanket she'd thrown at Frisco was on the floor. Picking it up, she folded it, then knelt to put it in the bottom drawer. What she couldn't see last night caused her to hesitate now. A framed picture of a man, a woman and twelve ragamuffin-looking boys stared out at her. The picture was eight-by-eleven, black-and-white, taken by a real photographer on the grounds of the Union Junction ranch. Though the boys looked rag-tag, it was clear that they were loved and happy. Everyone wore jeans, except the lady, who wore a Jackie Kennedy-style dress and gloves. She reminded Annabelle of Audrey Hepburn, with her big eyes and delicate frame.

If this was the Jefferson brothers' mother, she'd been quite a looker. She'd also been slightly built. Annabelle wrinkled her nose. She hadn't lost ten of the pounds she'd gained with Emmie. Multiply ten pounds by twelve kids.

And all the boys had that wiry, lean frame. "It's not fair. At least one of you could have been a mutant," she muttered. If the man in the picture was the father of the clan, he was tall, lean and handsome. Like all his offspring.

You'd think the Union Junction women would be throwing panties at the ranch windows every night.

Still, why waste a good pair of panties when none of the brothers was inclined to settle down? It was a little unsettling, because she knew Frisco had started knocking edges off her hard heart, softening it into a penetrable organ once again. If anything, this picture told her why she couldn't fall for him, even if she wanted to. She couldn't live up to the family frozen in time, captured in a perfect moment.

She put the frame away and stood up.

Frisco was leaning up on his elbows, watching her intently. "Find everything you need?"

"Not yet," she said, her nose in the air. She hated getting caught snooping and he darn well knew it, so he could just temper his sarcasm with a little sweetness today. "Have *you* found everything you need?"

"Not yet," he replied.

She crossed her arms. "I don't have to wait on you hand-and-foot. It's not a royal right ceded to you just because you were dumb enough to roll down a hill."

He scratched at the stubble on his face. "Calm down, Sparky. I apologize. I'm a little sensitive about…what's in that drawer."

"Fine. I'm a little sensitive about being snapped at."

His gaze roamed over her long skirt, boots and red sweater. "How'd you sleep?"

"Just like Emmie."

"I seem to have a beneficial effect on you Turn-berrys."

That she wasn't about to debate. "Do you want some orange juice? Breakfast?"

"I'm not very hungry. Thanks."

"Call me if you need something." She went to scoop up Emmie, who was starting to flail restlessly beside Frisco, a sure sign a bottle was needed.

"I'm sorry I teased you last night about the rivals across the street."

"It doesn't matter anymore."

She bent to pick up the baby. He reached out with a hand to halt her in mid-bend.

"I'll feed her. I've got nothing else to do, and I might as well be useful."

Her heart turned over. "Why are you being so nice about my baby?"

"Why not?"

"Because I really don't need your pity, and neither does Emmie. We're fine, Frisco, really fine on our own."

"I don't pity you. I'm feeling sorry for myself."

She stared into his dark eyes. "Because?"

"I don't really know. But I haven't held a baby in years, and I'm not ever going to hold one of my own, and the experience is far from killing me."

She couldn't say that yes, he would hold one of his own. He was pushing forty—slowly, but pushing it all the same—with no apparent inclination to do anything about getting babies. Her gaze slowly dropped, then returned to his. "Is it because of the picture? Is that why you keep it hidden?"

His eyes hooded suddenly. "I just want to feed Emmie, Annabelle. That's all I'm asking for. I have a strange feeling you're not going to be here much longer, and after that—and after my leg heals—I'm going to be back to work. Back to being myself. All this will be out of my system."

She wondered how he could know exactly what she'd been thinking. "Okay," she said, her arms hesitantly offering Emmie to him. "I'll bring you a bottle."

"And flip on that TV, if you don't mind. Emmie and I are going to watch something intelligent like football, aren't we, Emmie?" he cooed to the baby now curled into a tucked position on his chest. "Football strategy is good for you. Teamwork is key to a well-run home and business."

"Good grief." Annabelle left the room to hurry downstairs for the bottle. The man was a bit unhinged, even in an undrugged state.

"I THINK YOUR LITTLE birdy might be about ready to fly the coop," Jerry said to Delilah as they perched in his truck for a quick lunch break. "Not that I'm supposed to be giving you any info, mind you."

"I was afraid of that." Delilah sighed. "Annabelle's my rolling stone. The only reason she hung around the salon as long as she did was because she felt guilty about Emmie. Figured it was best for the baby to have a chance to know her father. Annabelle's real sensitive about that type of thing since she lost her father last year.''

''Is that why she looks so uncomfortable all the time? Like she can't light for more than five minutes?''

''She's still grieving, that's for certain. And trying to figure out her place in the world. Annabelle doesn't really belong in a small town, I'm afraid. She's a big-city girl, the daughter of Jason Turnberry, wine magnate. She's got a ton of money, though she's refusing to touch much of it right now while she's trying to figure out where she fits and what she could make of herself without family money. I've often been thankful for her decision to live more simply, because I believe if that pond scum, Tom, had ever figured out who she was, he'd have stuck on her like a leech. And he didn't love her. Not even a little, so I'm grateful she's smart enough to try to find her own way.''

''It's good to know who one is in life.''

''Yes.'' Delilah nodded. ''And Annabelle never had the chance to figure it out. Her mother was some society dame who didn't want her, so Jason Turnberry raised her. Only he became ill in the last ten years of his life, starting about the time Annabelle would have just about graduated college. She came home and spent the last years of her father's life nursing him. He was her best friend, her only family, and he left Annabelle his company." Delilah shrugged. "So when she lost her father, she lost her whole person."

Jerry sighed. "It's too bad she won't find herself in time. I do believe I saw a twinkle in Frisco's eye for her."

"Well, if he twinkled, she'd sure put out the flame. Besides, she doesn't belong here, Jerry. And if I'm not mistaken, these boys are somewhat emotionally devastated themselves. No bonding ability at all. A lot of cock, a bit of bull and too much story, if you know what I mean. No feminine touch to rein all that in."

"I don't reckon you put two people in the same boat unless they both know how to row."

"And how to swim if the boats tips over." Delilah stood, brushing crumbs from her jeans. "I'm just learning a few new strokes myself since my sister came to town."

"You'll outlast her."

She shook her head. "I have no idea what makes Marvella tick. But if grit gets me any points, I'll be standing no matter what she does. You don't happen to know where I can find a cowboy who can stay on the meanest bull in Texas, do you?"

"I'm well past my youth, Delilah, though you

know I'd sure try to stick in the saddle. Why do you need a cowboy?''

''Every year the town holds a big fair, and one of the draws is bull-riding. The cowboy with the best time wins the purse. I sure could use the purse, now that Marvella's managed to draw my business down so much. We've always won, and I've always been able to give the purse to charity. This year, I'm sorry to say, my business is the charity.'' She looked at him sadly. ''If I want to keep these girls on, I'm going to need some cash.''

''Delilah, I'd be happy—''

She held up a hand. ''Thank you, Jerry, but it's a resourceful woman who rides the waves of luck, be it high or low tide. If it's time for the Lonely Hearts Salon to go out on ebb tide, so be it. But I plan to pay my girls something.''

He pursed his lips. ''What kind of riding is it?''

''Ugly. Because you have to have a bull that doesn't just dance around like a youthful grandma. You have to have one that's full of fire, as that's what draws the audience. And my bull is Blood-thirsty Black.''

''Oh. And Marvella's?''

''Bad-Ass Blue. She just got him last year— bought him from the best-scoring cowboy at the Fort Worth rodeo.''

''She really does have it in for you, doesn't she?''

''Every bit, every step of the way.''

"Ever think about getting out of her way?"

"Nope." She shook her head at him and grinned. "I was there first. I'm older. It's my town. If one of us goes, it ain't gonna be me."

"That-a-girl." He squinted toward the dam where the Jefferson brothers were busy replacing sandbags in the shoring that had slipped in the night. "You know what sticks in a saddle the best, Delilah?"

"What?"

"A tall tale. Every word bigger and braver than the last. A lot of cock, a bit of bull and too much story, as you put it."

"The Jefferson brothers?"

"I heard one of them mention he was thinking about trying the rodeo circuit."

She watched them for a few moments. "Nah," she said after a while. "They've already got one man down. Whoever rides Bloodthirsty Black is likely to get busted up. I couldn't do that to them."

"You just don't want to ask them because you'd be asking for something for yourself. These men know what it means to try to keep a business afloat, Delilah."

"I know. But I'm admiring Annabelle these days, Jerry. I'm going to figure out something on my own."

Chapter Ten

Around nightfall, Laredo and Tex went to town with Jerry to pick up the ladies and haul them back to the ranch for dinner.

"They sure have been good sports about their vacation getting screwed up," Laredo said.

"I may miss them when they go," Tex agreed. "A few of them, anyway."

Jerry grunted from his place at the wheel. The brothers looked at each other.

"Maybe this means we need a woman or two at the ranch. Liven things up a bit," Tex said.

"We could get some dogs if all we wanted was to liven things up a bit," Laredo pointed out. "Although that Katy Goodnight gal kind of caught my eye. I like the way she mops."

"Oh, now there's a proposal. 'Hang out with me at the ranch so I can watch you mop.'" Tex and Jerry had a good laugh at Laredo's expense.

"I like the way she moves her tush. Back and

forth, side to side. Then north and south. Her dark hair flops around in that long ponytail and—what?'' Laredo stopped as both men were staring at him incredulously.

''You've got the hots for her,'' Tex said.

''Uh-uh. Liking to watch a woman mop is not having the hots for her,'' Laredo argued.

''He may have a point. It sounds more like he has a fetish for clean floors.''

''And even if I do have a fetish for clean floors, which I do not—is it a crime to like the way a woman moves, I ask you? Is that any better or worse than having an over-excited enthusiasm for manure and buds that never open for you?''

Tex stiffened, insulted. ''Any day now, one of those roses is going to open, Laredo. It's going to be lush and beautiful and fragrant—''

''Jeez, Tex, why don't you just get a woman?'' Laredo couldn't explain why he was so annoyed, except that he hadn't liked being teased. That didn't make him a chauvinist or anything. She could have been wiping tables and he probably would have been just as—

An unpleasant thought hit him. ''There's a possibility that I don't know what a woman's for beyond housekeeping, and the obvious,'' Laredo said slowly. ''I never thought about it before. All I remember of mom is her cleaning the house. She was happy about it. She sang a lot.''

"She could pipe up on Dad a bit, too," Tex said wistfully. "Boy, he didn't like it when she was upset with him."

"No, he didn't."

"I just don't have her magic touch with roses," Tex said with a sigh.

"It hasn't felt like the Union Junction Ranch in a long time," Laredo said. "More like Malfunction Junction, just like the townfolks say. Seems more and more as if they're right."

Tex nodded. "Yep. That's what we are. Malfunction Junction."

Jerry didn't say a word as he drove. Laredo decided there wasn't anything else to say. He was feeling melancholy and reminiscent. The Lonely Hearts ladies had shown him one thing—life at the ranch was pretty stale. He'd been ready to scratch his itch a long time ago, and head out to see the world, starting in the Appalachian mountains, maybe head up the eastern seaboard.

It would be hard on Mason, what with Frisco being off his leg for a while. But there was no time like the present for a man to do something big with himself, and as soon as winter lightened up a little, he was going to leave.

ANNABELLE GAVE EMMIE her last bottle for the evening, then put her in a pretty white sleeper. "You're such an angel," she told the baby. "I love you."

Emmie seemed to nuzzle her back. Annabelle knew it was too soon for her daughter to really react to her, but still, it felt good. And she looked forward to the future, when Emmie would recognize her instantly.

For a moment, she thought of Tom, and what he'd chosen to miss out on. She felt sorry for Emmie, who would never know her daddy. "I had a wonderful daddy, your grandfather. You would have been the apple of his eye."

That made her sad, so she tucked her baby onto her chest and headed up the stairs to put Emmie to bed.

"It's about time," Frisco complained as soon as she entered. "Don't you think Emmie should get to bed earlier?"

"I beg your pardon? Are you trying to tell me you know what's best for my daughter?"

"No. I missed her, though. Come here, little bit, and let me hold you."

Frisco stretched out his arms to take the baby, and it was all Annabelle could do not to let the tears she felt stinging show. She surrendered the baby, watching her tiny daughter be engulfed by two big hands.

"I heard you're leaving tomorrow," Frisco said

"From who?" She felt surprised and embarrassed. She'd wanted to slip out without him knowing.

"You said goodbye to Delilah. She was pretty

shook up about it, and she told all the girls so they'd know to say goodbye to you tomorrow." He laid the baby down beside him, tucking a blanket around her, before giving Annabelle a full-on stare. "I figured I'd say my goodbye tonight."

"I see. Well, it's a bit awkward." It was a lot awkward.

"Were you going to say goodbye to me?"

She avoided his gaze. "Not necessarily."

"That would have hurt my feelings."

She still didn't look at him. "That wouldn't have been my intention."

"Maybe not. I'm just telling you that I wouldn't have liked that at all."

"I'm sorry."

"Please look at me."

It was hard, because she wanted to—and yet, she was so afraid. There were things she wanted to see in his eyes, and yet, those same things she didn't want to see. How could she explain to him what she really didn't understand about herself?

"Annabelle."

Slowly, she turned at the command in his tone. "Yes?" she whispered.

"Kiss me."

"I can't."

"Because?"

She could barely hold his gaze. Even her hands

were trembling. "Because I'm…it's not the right thing to do."

"Can't take advantage of a man with a broken leg?"

He was trying to lighten the mood, but when it came to the idea of kissing him, she couldn't take it as a simple matter of swapping saliva. "Why do you want to kiss me?"

"Because I have the strangest feeling that I'll always regret it if I don't. You…pull me to you in some way I can't quite explain. And I think you feel that pull, too."

"I don't."

"Not at all?"

She lowered her gaze.

"I understand about Emmie's father, Annabelle. I know it's too soon for you. I'm not trying to rush you. It's like having the answer to a question, and I guess I want the answer."

"You scare me," she murmured.

"In a good way?"

"Is there a good way to scare someone?" She stared at him, curious.

"Well, you scare me a little, too. But I think it's called attraction. And I understand you want to leave. But I'm more scared that you won't kiss me." He caught her fingers in his as she stood beside the bed. "I really, really got scared when I found out you were leaving tomorrow. Tell a man who's got a busted leg that the woman he's been mulling over kissing for two days is leaving. That's almost cruel. I couldn't come find you; I couldn't run you down and grab you like I wanted to. I had to wait, and hope that you'd come upstairs to put Emmie in my bed. It was torture, Annabelle.''

She hadn't meant to torture him. She was tortured enough for both of them. He'd been the one to turn away last night, which had hurt more than she could have imagined.

And yet, she was touched that Frisco had wanted to come to her for this kiss he wanted so badly. He'd admitted to feeling some of the pain she was feeling, which made her feel much less alone. ''I felt abandoned,'' she whispered.

''I know. I thought about it later and knew I'd screwed up. But you were gone this morning before I could tell you, and then I heard you were thinking of leaving....''

Neither of them were certain of the proper steps in the dance. He hadn't meant to make her feel deserted—it was just too soon after Tom's abandonment, and she'd felt that painful feeling again. Her father's death had left her feeling alone and shipwrecked, too.

A kiss, nothing more. As Frisco pointed out, he was in no position to chase her down if kissing made her more nervous than she could handle.

A kiss. Swapping saliva. Sucking face. No need to make more of it than it was.

And Frisco was basically promising her that he wouldn't leave her out there by herself. If she was ever going to move forward with her life, she had to get over being afraid of every lonesome shadow.

Slowly, Annabelle moved her face toward his, startled when Frisco removed his fingers from hers to cradle her face in his hands as gently as if she were Emmie. She nearly sighed with the pleasure of it.

He touched his lips to hers, and she sank onto the bed beside him, every fiber of her body relaxing toward him. Ever so unnoticeably, he increased the pressure until he was no longer just touching her lips, but a part of her.

It felt so good.

He pulled back, and her mind cried out, Don't stop!

"All right?"

All she could do was nod. Beside them, Emmie's soft breathing hung in the room.

This time, Annabelle moved toward him, placing her lips on his, trusting, wanting, seeking. His hands tightened on her face, pulling her toward him. Her knees went limp, so she drew her legs up onto the bed. Facing him, she leaned into him more, and when his arms went around her, it was as if her whole body sighed with recognition.

Heat and passion and warmth. All the things Tom had never given her spun through her mind. Closing her eyes, she reveled in the magic of the moment.

And when Frisco pulled away from her and moved her head down onto his chest, she leaned against him, relaxing as her hammering heart slowed, content to take the shelter he was offering.

Nothing had ever felt so good in her whole life.

And yet, it was the worst thing she could have discovered. Real passion. True heat. Something that came along maybe once, twice in a lifetime, with a special person.

She might never know it again in her life.

WHEN SHE AWAKENED the next morning, she found herself still tucked up against Frisco's chest. Fully dressed. He couldn't be comfortable like that, especially with his broken leg.

She hadn't seen him take any pain pills since the first night. Couldn't blame what happened on happy tablets.

"Time to go?"

She turned at his deep voice. "After I feed Emmie."

He was silent for a long moment. "You're special, Annabelle. Don't forget it."

She had forgotten it, and more, after Tom had deserted her. "Thank you, Frisco. You are, too."

He made her feel good about herself. He made her feel special.

She couldn't wait to get out of his room, and out of his house.

"Promise me you'll call if you need anything. Anything at all."

She nodded. "I will."

She wouldn't.

Last night's kiss hung between them. She couldn't look at him. Without a glance, she picked Emmie up and hurried to the door.

"Goodbye, Annabelle."

"Goodbye, Frisco."

She left with a stolen glance at him. With two days stubble on his face he looked rakish, especially with his shirt off and his long body obvious under the white sheet. She'd lain quite happily on that broad chest.

Oh, my Lord. If I don't go now, I'll beg him pitifully to keep me and Emmie forever, she thought.

Hadn't Frisco said he wasn't interested in children or settling down? That he had all the family he needed?

Whatever was between them had to be attraction. She could live with that. Attraction could be recovered from, like a case of head lice.

Becoming dependent on him, when he'd clearly outlined his life, was not what she was going to do.

She'd already been dumped once, and she had no intention of putting herself in that position again.

But there had been one really good thing about Frisco that made her see her life in a new light. She could live through anything: colic, grouchy cowboys, single parenthood. Cooking. Ice storms.

Now she had known kindness from a man besides her father. And real passion.

She felt herself changing, like sun moving shadows away from rocks.

Instead of continuing her old habit of moving on, she was going back to the Lonely Hearts Salon. Not to work, but to cross that damn street and walk right in the door of the Never Lonely Cut-n-Gurls. With Emmie.

She was going to ask to speak to Tom.

He was going to meet Emmie face-to-face. Emmie was not a monster. She was not at fault. If an ornery cowboy could take a shine to her little baby, then Emmie was bound to catch the heart of the most hard-hearted male.

Maybe not Tom's heart, but that was to be determined. Annabelle accepted this might be the case. But Tom was by golly going to see Emmie. Emmie was going to have her chance with her blood father.

And if Tom refused to see her—and Emmie—that was fine, too. She would slap him with a paternity suit so fast it would make his sunshine-blond head swim. She didn't need the money. It was something she hadn't thought of before, because she'd been running from rejection.

Frisco had taught her that she had no reason to run from Tom's rejection. Frisco was better-looking, more successful—and unless she badly miscalculated what had been under that sheet before she'd tossed the blanket on him, had about four inches on Tom in a very manly place.

And Tom couldn't kiss worth a damn.

Frisco had found her desirable. He gave her confidence. She'd fight for Emmie's chance to know her father. Paternity suit, visiting rights, whatever.

Like Marvella, Annabelle could be a pain. She'd simply be a boil under Tom's behind he couldn't get away from. Until he saw his daughter, Annabelle wouldn't rest.

And if he didn't want her after that, so be it. But she'd do her duty as a mother. It wasn't revenge she was seeking and she didn't want Tom back. So far from it. Child support was the minimum Emmie should get from him. Acknowledgment at the maximum. A father's love only a prayer.

It took two to tango, and she was ready to dance. Thanks to Frisco.

An hour later, when she'd packed herself and Emmie into Jerry's truck, she hugged and kissed her friends. "I'll see you in a few days," she told them. "I've changed my mind about leaving town for good. I've changed my mind about a lot of things."

"That's my girl," Delilah said. "I always knew you had grit."

Annabelle glanced up toward the upper story of the house. If she hadn't known it was impossible, since Frisco couldn't stand up by himself, she would have thought she saw his shadow in the window, behind the curtain.

Just in case, she waved.

The shadow didn't move.

Wishful thinking. "Tell Frisco thanks for everything. Funny that none of us ever laid eyes on Mason, since he was the reason we came out here in the first place."

"Ah, well," Delilah said. "We never know what the future holds."

Jerry closed the cab door. Annabelle buckled herself in, with Emmie in a car seat between her and Jerry. Glancing back up at the window, she saw that the shadow was gone. But the sun had moved, as well, and if she'd learned anything on her time at the Union Junction Ranch, it was that she'd never chase shadows again.

Chapter Eleven

Four hours after Annabelle had left, Frisco's room filled with the rest of the Lonely Hearts ladies.

For his part, Frisco, unused to having women in his room, decided to pull the sheet as high over his waist as he could. There was some appreciative eyeing going on, and while he once upon a time would have eyed appreciatively back, he was feeling a bit more unfriendly than usual.

He missed Emmie in the bed beside him. That little short-term carpet-grabber had been quite a comfort, once she'd stopped griping about her stomach pains. He sure hoped those cramps didn't return.

He wasn't happy about Annabelle leaving, but women were known to be notoriously headstrong about whatever they decided to do. A mental shrug and a curse was all he was going to spare on that.

Besides, he had all these women in his room, and he wasn't sure what they wanted. It felt rather as though a jury had assembled at the foot of his bed, catching him out when he'd been scrolling the TV channels hoping for a glimpse of a better football game or Pamela Anderson to take his mind off his leg, the missing baby and the woman he'd kissed last night.

No big deal.

"What's up, ladies?"

"We're leaving," Delilah said.

"Any particular reason?" He didn't think he could handle pounding his brothers if they'd gotten out of line. On a good day, he would enjoy the exercise; today, he just wanted to lie still and debate the world's existence as it centered in his leg.

"All good things must come to an end," Delilah said with a grin. "We've got to get on to the next leg of our journey."

Talk of legs at this point only brought a wince. He tried to concentrate on being a good host. "I thought you were on vacation."

"A vacation should be a journey, if possible, while being a fun trip."

He squinted at her. "Am I getting a lecture? I should know, so I can pay attention."

She smiled at him. "You've had your mind on other things."

Oh. Possibly she was pointing out his interest in Annabelle. Could be she meant he was mainly focused on himself. He wasn't sure where she was heading with this, but he looked at her with alert, careful eyes. "Good luck on your journey. I take it you're looking for something. Maybe you'll find it."

Her gaze, and seventeen others, focused on him as he lay helpless in the bed. The sensation made his scalp crawl. They were smiling at him.

These women wanted something. And he didn't think they wanted the biggest ménage-à-plenty Texas might have ever seen. "Ah, Delilah, why are you smiling at me like you've got a secret only recently unclassified by a rogue feminist group?"

"We'd like to give you a parting gift," Delilah said. "Something to make you feel better."

"I feel fine—"

"When we get through with you, you're going to feel better."

One of the ladies closed the door.

He resisted the unmanly, unexplainable urge to shout for Tex and Laredo. These women looked way too happy about whatever they were going to do.

Four approached the bed. He clutched the sheet.

"Hold still, Frisco," Delilah practically cooed. And she pulled out the biggest pair of pointy scissors he'd ever seen. On the opposite side of the bed, the buzz of an electric razor punctuated his apprehension.

He was trapped with women whose goal was to whip him into shape.

And there was nothing he could do about it.

TWO HOURS LATER, Frisco closed his eyes in relief. They were done, finally satisfied. Every pore of his body was warm with relaxation. He'd been cut, clipped, trimmed, massaged; in short, totally tamed. Hair styled, stubble gone, nails buffed. His cast was signed in colorful pens by all eighteen women. The sheets had been changed. He'd been lifted from them by Tex and Laredo, whom Delilah called to the scene.

Tex and Laredo had left—the traitors!—laughing at him as if he were a prize poodle getting a blue-ribbon grooming.

Even his room was clean, not a speck of dust anywhere. Katy and Delilah had taken down the blue-checked drapes in his room and washed them. Lemon-oil permeated the air, mingling with the smell of clean sheets and body lotion.

"Ah-h-h" was all he could say. At this point, if they'd wanted to put beads in his hair or a tattoo on his back, he probably wouldn't argue. "Thank you. Thank you. Thank you."

"You're welcome," Delilah said. "Thank you for having us out."

"Oh, it was no trouble at all," Frisco said, feeling less like a prisoner and more like a prince. "You just come on back anytime. Anytime at all."

His eyelids closed. He couldn't help himself. Reaching up, he felt where the hair used to brush his collar. Neck shaved nicely. And his hair no longer fell into his eyes.

Those ladies certainly knew what they were doing.

A sudden itch hit his leg, and he reached down to scratch it without opening his eyes. His fingers contacted something not part of the cast. Opening his eyes, he pulled it out.

It was a business card. Pink, with purple lettering.

Lonely Hearts Beauty Salon.
Let us take care of you.

Well, he wouldn't be driving that far for a haircut every three weeks.

His eyes snapped open.

But he might for another reason.

MIMI HEARD THE SOUND of her father opening the front door. She listened, wondering who would be visiting. Probably the deputy, or some of the other officers, as they knew her father was at home today. The flooding had required his attention around the clock, and he was tired. He seemed to get tired more quickly lately, and it worried her.

He was not the young man he'd once been, and he worked darn hard.

After a few minutes, when she didn't hear the sound of men's deep voices, she went downstairs.

To her surprise, all the Lonely Hearts women were talking to her father.

"Hi," she said to the room at large. "Is there something wrong?"

"We just came to say goodbye," Delilah told her. "We didn't want to leave without letting the sheriff know we were going."

"Oh." Mimi supposed that was fair enough. She couldn't say she was sad. Mason was due back soon, and if all this crew was cleared out—particularly the too-cute Annabelle and her precious bundle of joy— Mimi wouldn't mind. It would make matters less complicated, because Helga was supposed to be here tomorrow. Helga, not Olga.

Mason would be so pleased. Julia said she'd sent the perfect woman to fit Mimi's description of what Mason needed.

Delilah, her dad and the other women looked at Mimi, obviously waiting for something. She quickly reviewed her manners. Uh-oh, lacking, once again, in her pursuit of Mason's happiness.

"All of you did so much for Union Junction," she said sincerely. "I know my father has probably said it, but the shopkeepers said many times that if you ever decided to move your beauty salon here, they'd welcome you with open arms and help you make a success of it. And in this town, that's saying a lot. They don't often offer welcome with open arms."

Particularly to a bunch of pretty women, Mimi thought.

"We were proud to assist. We've enjoyed being here. It felt like our own town," Delilah said.

"I'm sorry it didn't work out. The housekeeper's position, I mean." She tried to look sorry and might have made it, since her father's gaze was approving.

"Oh, that's all right. That's part of the interviewing process. There's no guarantee of being hired. But we had a great time with the men over there. Sorry we missed Mason, though."

"Yes, well, he won't be back for a few more days," Mimi said hurriedly. "I'll tell him all about what nice ladies his e-mail advertisement brought to town." Although when *she* told the story, none of *them* would be man-magnets.

Storytelling license, the discretion of the teller.

"We owe the first wonderful days of our vacation to you, Mimi. In a way, if it hadn't been for you, we might still be adding up vacation days," Katy Goodnight said.

"We'd like to do something for you," Delilah added. "To thank you."

"No need. We should be thanking you," Mimi said, her manners now silver-shiny for her father's sake. "Truly."

He nodded at Delilah. Delilah turned to look at Mimi. Uh-oh, secret signals.

"Our only way of thanking anyone is to give

them a makeover," Delilah continued. "And since your father mentioned you have a date tonight—with a lawyer fellow, right?—we'd like to give you the works. If you'd let us."

Mimi's jaw sagged a bit. Her father beamed.

"Uh—" she stammered.

"A few highlights, some pretty makeup, a little sparkle on the fingers and toes…what do you say, Mimi? You're beautiful already, but we'd love to make tonight really special for you."

Glancing down at her blue jeans and boots, Mimi didn't have to reach up to feel that her hair had long since grown out of any type of style. It was cowgirl-casual. Her makeup was Maybelline-over-my-dead-body. Her perfume was eau-de-pasture, and her skin was best described as cat-tongue rough.

She didn't give a flying cow patty about the lawyer coming to see her father tonight. But Mason would be home soon—and if these ladies thought they were miracle-workers, who was she to stand in the way of the great white light?

"You know, Delilah, that sounds wonderful," she said. "I'd really, really love to take you up on your oh-so-kind offer."

Wouldn't Mason be surprised?

THE MIRACLE THAT THEY wrought on her was nothing short of well, glamorous, Mimi decided. "Your shop must stay full of customers," she told them, looking at herself in awe. "You must have a waiting list a mile long. Thank you so much! I never dreamed I could look like this."

Delilah gave her a pleased once-over as she packed away a large cosmetics case, rollers and nail polishes. "We don't have as many customers as we like."

"Well, I second the invitation from our community, then. Come here and open up a shop!" She twirled her skirt in front of the cheval mirror. A skirt! Twinkly red sequins adorned the seriously-short skirt, black sequins adorned the heart-shaped bodice, and a long black lace length of fabric with more sequins lay across her shoulders and hung delicately to her hands, keeping the ensemble from looking scandalous. Sexy, but not scandalous. Just right for an evening with someone her father wanted her to entertain.

"We can't come here," Katy said. "We're going to stay and fight."

"Fight?" Now there was a word Mimi had some passing acquaintance with. "What kind of fight?"

"Oh, metaphorically speaking. Never mind that," Delilah said, brushing off the question. She smiled at Mimi. "We have to go now, but have a good time."

Mimi hugged Delilah. "You're like my fairy godmother."

"I hope the mystery man is a prince, then."

"Oh. Him. Yeah, maybe he will be." Too bad Mason can't see this dress. It would knock his boots off!

Of course, there was no need for drastic measures. She didn't even know why she cared about what His Highness the Hard-Headed thought.

"Goodbye," she said, walking the ladies to the door. "Stop back by some day." Not too soon, of course, because Helga was due to come tomorrow, and she didn't want anyone's feelings hurt. "Bye!"

"Bye!" the group called back. It was like watching a camp retreat, Mimi mused, as the ladies put their suitcases on the porch and went outside.

Thirty minutes later, they loaded up into various trucks, driven by the Jefferson brothers, and headed out. For the bus station, likely.

The phone rang, and she jerked it up, still amazed by the woman staring back at her in the mirror. How did those women get her hair to curl like that? So sexy and feminine! It was almost like not looking at herself, but someone soft and gentle and desirable. "Hello?"

"Mimi, Frisco."

She frowned at his growl. "So?"

"So you remember when you said you weren't helping us out while Mason was gone?"

Her lower lip stuck out. "Yeah?"

"Well, you done a fine job of keeping your word, but now you're going to have to come over."

Not in these heels, buster. Delilah's crew had talked her into pantyhose—disgusting!—and high heels. The dress and heels were to be shipped to the Lonely Hearts Salon after tonight. She wasn't going to risk ruining this get-up just because Frisco had been careless. "I can't. Can it wait until…tomorrow?" When Cinderella will be wearing jeans and boots again and not borrowed girlie glam?

"There's a woman here—in my room, I might add—who seems to think she's applying for a job," he said tersely.

Mimi blinked. It couldn't be any of Delilah's girls—they'd all just left. Annabelle was long gone. "You shouldn't let strangers in the house, Frisco. Anyway, there's no position to apply for. I thought we settled that a few days ago."

"We did. This lady says—in very broken English—that you sent for her. Her name is Helga."

"Oh! Helga! Why didn't you say so? I'll be right there. You be nice to her, Frisco. Just because you've got a broken leg is no reason to be a sourpuss."

She hung up, gave herself one last glance in the mirror—and a fluff under her long, curly hair just for fun. She called to her dad that she was leaving and decided that this once she'd drive next door.

"WHAT TOOK YOU SO LONG?"

Mimi glared at Frisco, prone in the bed with a

very large, very old woman sitting next to him on a chair she'd moved quite close to the bed—almost as if she were afraid he might escape.

"Why are you dressed like that? You look like a showgirl," he complained.

"A showgirl?"

"Yeah, the kind that—"

"Sh! I'm sure you have wide experience in the different varieties of showgirls, Frisco. We need not hear about your downfall." She pinched the big toe of his bad leg surreptitiously and smiled at the grim-faced woman tucked right up beside Frisco's bed.

"It's *so* nice to meet you," she said with a sugary smile. "Welcome to Union Junction, Helga."

"Tank you," Helga said without smiling.

She was *perfect.* As nice as Delilah's crew had been, this was the housekeeper Mason needed.

"You're hired," she said.

"Tank you," Helga replied, her eyes gleaming as she looked down at Frisco. Mimi pinched his toe again, enjoying his smothered curse.

That would teach him to call her a showgirl.

Chapter Twelve

"I'm home!"

A man's voice from downstairs brought a gasp from Mimi. "Mason!"

She tore downstairs, fluffing her hair one last time before bursting from the stairwell. He was looking through the mail.

"Hi, Mason," she said.

He glanced up, did a double take.

Mimi's heart soared.

"What happened to you?" he asked.

Her heart crash-landed. "What?"

He stared at her, his gaze taking in the oh-so-short skirt, the high, strappy heels and then the curls. Scratching his head, he said, "Let me guess. Costume party?"

Drawing herself up tall, she forced herself to act as if she didn't want to kick him in the shin. "Not tonight. Maybe in October, though. Mason, the housekeeper is upstairs with Frisco."

"Great." His head swivelled as he glanced around the den and kitchen, his gaze much more interested and approving than he'd been to her. "New curtains. Flowers. Mm, and something's in the oven."

Delilah and her crew must have put something in for the guys before they left. Mimi stood statue-still as Mason looked at his feet. "And vacuumed, even." He looked up at her, his eyes full of…surprise. "You were right," he said, not bothered at all to have to make the admission. "We did need a housekeeper around here. She's awesome, Mimi."

Her heart crumbled, she wasn't about to tell him that Helga wasn't the cause of his newfound contentment. He looked too happy, and it was so great to have one of her plans go right instead of backfiring like a bad firework.

"I'm glad you…think she'll work out for you."

"Well, if she did all this, then yeah, it's going to be great!"

His enthusiasm was heartening, yet it was killing her. Why not that glow in his eyes for her?

"I've got to go," she said. "I'll see you later."

"What's the hurry? Stay and have dinner with us. It smells great."

Stay and have dinner with me and the boys, she wanted to mimic. She looked down at her sparkly nails and her gleaming red toenails. "I can't. Thanks, though, Mason. Good night."

She went to the front door, turning at the last moment. He was looking through the mail again.

"By the way, her name is Helga."

"What? Oh, okay."

He nodded, as if it mattered. But now she knew it didn't. Mason didn't care who took care of his hearth and home. She was his friend, and she always would be.

She left, her heart broken.

MASON COULD HARDLY WAIT until the front door closed behind Mimi. He'd nearly dropped his teeth when he looked up and saw her! His heart thundered and his blood felt as if it was going to pound out of his ears.

It had been totally obvious that she had a date, and he wasn't about to let on how much that bugged him. She'd never bothered to get all babed up for him, though. Whoever it was, he had to be someone she was set on impressing. He'd never seen her in high heels. Not even at the prom, damn it. She'd worn a long dress and her boots underneath.

His brow furrowed. In fact, if they hadn't swum in the swimming hole over the years, he'd never even have seen her toenails. And there she was, with some red glittery paint peeping out of shoes that looked as if they belonged on one of Laredo's dates.

He didn't want Mimi giving another man glittery toes and heart-shaped cleavage.

Damn and blast. More had changed around here than the curtains.

"Mason? Is that you?" Frisco called.

He sounded edgy. "Be right up," Mason answered.

Needing it bad, he grabbed a beer to keep him company. He'd swallowed half of it before he crested the stairwell, and it was a good thing, too, otherwise he would have spewed it.

Frisco had what looked like a busted leg—surely there was a costume party Mimi and Frisco weren't telling him about—and an elderly female warden was frisking his brother.

"What's...going on?" Mason asked weakly.

"She—Ms. Helga—wants me to change the channel. She doesn't think watching *Sex Slaves from Outer Space* is good for a man with a broken leg."

"Why not?"

"Hell if I know!" Frisco finally gave up and surrendered the remote. The channel was changed to a cooking show.

"Do something," Frisco pleaded.

"What the hell happened to you?" Mason demanded, frowning at the leg cast.

"Ch-ch," Ms. Helga said.

"Uh, sorry." Mason looked at his brother, who looked imprisoned. Maybe Ms. Helga was only efficient like this because Frisco was laid up. All the other changes he'd seen in the house so far were positive ones. If they had to tone down the swearing, that would probably be best for all of them.

"Do something," Frisco implored.

"I think…I'll go get another beer." He headed downstairs, his brain too twisted by Mimi's get-up to deal with Frisco's moaning right now. Ms. Helga was obviously very conscientious about her work. Conscientious wouldn't kill Frisco.

Besides, dinner smelled *heavenly*.

AN HOUR LATER, MASON thought he was going to heave his dinner; he was outside counting calves and a red Ferrari pulled into Mimi's driveway.

He ducked behind some big-bodied heifers to spy unashamedly. Ten minutes later, out she came in her red dress, with a big lunkhead opening the car door for her. "Dressing to match the car. I'll have to remember that," he muttered to himself.

Since he had a white truck, she'd have to wear something white to go out with him. Very white. With white shoes. And white pantyhose, he told himself in a very smart-alecky, discontented inner voice. No, make that white stockings, garter belt, and thong. Gotta have the thong. Waited a long time to have the thong.

He heard Mimi's delighted giggle float on the wind as the Ferrari roared past.

Would like the thong between my teeth, he told himself. What am I thinking?

This was practically his little sister he was thinking pornographic thoughts about. This was his best gal pal, his comrade-in-pranks. She could date if she wanted. It shouldn't throw him. That was it. She'd just thrown him with the new look and the Ferrari.

Then he sighed. He'd known for a long time that Mimi was restless. She was only staying in Union Junction because of her father. If her mother hadn't deserted them for the bright lights of Hollywood— an act for which Mimi despised her mother—Mimi herself would have been a disappearing act only rivaled by the great Houdini.

"Damn, damn, damn." He kicked at a fence post that had a lean to it, righted it and worked it farther into the ground.

Then he stopped, horrified.

He had no idea what she was wearing under that dress.

It could be the white thong of his fantasies.

The skirt was undeniably short. A woman wouldn't wear granny panties under something that delicate.

Or…or…

It could be not a damn thing at all.

"Mason!" his brother yelled out an upstairs window. "Mason, help!"

He saw Frisco wrestling with his jailer, back-lit by the light in the room. But he had much bigger problems than Frisco's sense of injured independence. "Shut up, Frisco! Do you want the whole damn countryside to hear you?"

"Yes!"

The window closed with a crack. Mason shook his head and went inside the house.

Surely Mimi wouldn't fall for a man who drove a wimpy car like the one she'd gone off in. "City dude," he muttered. "Mimi'll never fall for that scarecrow-dressing."

And if she did—which she wouldn't—he'd be the first one to throw rice at her wedding.

Wedding dresses were white. *That* would match my truck, he thought, mulling over the startling complexity of his undiscovered feelings for Mimi.

But knowing Mimi, she'd probably wear black just to be different—or annoying, depending on how one saw it—so he could sit in the front row and smile at the sad sack who eventually got duped into marrying her.

FRISCO WAS READY TO KILL Mimi Cannady. Helga had made him her special project, and though she meant well, he was sleep-deprived and hallucinating. He didn't trust the woman. No, that was too strong a word. He wasn't comfortable with the woman manning his room. Oh, occasionally she left to clean or cook or do whatever. And Mason seemed as happy as Mason could seem. Tex and Laredo said they preferred to stay out of it and remained un moved by his complaints.

But he missed Emmie, and all the spoiling he'd got from Annabelle. Now that was how a man should recover. Little Emmie relaxed him, and Annabelle had made him believe there was life with a broken leg.

Helga made him wish for the kind of conscience that would allow him to slip his pain medication into her water glass. She could sleep peacefully until his leg healed—and he could tell Mason that Mimi had hired a cadaver for a housekeeper.

It was all Mimi's fault. They didn't need a damn housekeeper.

He said as much to Mason when he came up to visit the next day. Helga was off getting him some lunch, so Frisco took the opportunity to make his case.

"There's plenty of changes around here, all for the better, I might add. No one would call this Malfunction Junction anymore," Mason said with pleasure.

Yeah, they could. It was. Likely it always would be. "Mason, I think Mimi pulled a fast one on you," Frisco began.

"Like what?"

"Like…this Helga."

"Favorably recommended by Mimi's friend, Julia Finehurst from the Honey-Do Agency."

"Yeah, well, remember the ad you posted on the Internet? It said over forty or something like that, right? Not forty times two?"

"Are you discriminating against the elderly?" Mason asked with surprise.

Mason's shame-on-you tone grated on Frisco. "No. But, okay, what about the 'must not be offended by swearing' part? Every time one of us drops a minorly offensive word, even something so simple as *bird crap,* we get 'Ch-ch.'''

"It's just as well to say *bird doo* when Helga's around."

If Frisco's leg wasn't broken, he'd have slapped his elder brother with the sense he was badly lacking. "And the part about not minding big animals? She saw that bull get loose to try to jump up on the new red cow and nearly lost her dentures."

"She thought that he was going to hurt the female. She was just trying to point out something she thought was going wrong. Wouldn't you want to know if something bad was happening? Frankly, I find a pair of sharp eyes around here comforting. Besides, who's going to look after you? We can't lose a man to baby-sit you."

"I was in *better* hands," Frisco said, surly-toned.

"What?"

Frisco shook his head, unwilling to bring up Annabelle and Emmie.

"You know, Frisco, it's past time you and I cleared the air between us." Mason put a boot up on the foot of the bed, leaning forward. "You've been at me like a bad-tempered jackass for months. It's worse than ever since I got back. What's eating you?"

"I can't imagine."

"I can't, either. But I'm about tired of putting up with it."

"So shoot me and put me out of my misery."

"Don't think I wouldn't if I had a tranquilizing gun. The next time I'm at the vet, I may borrow one. I'll tell him we've got a big ornery jackass that won't simmer down."

"You wouldn't."

Mason cocked a brow at him. "Get off of Helga's back. She's done a lot around here."

Then he left the room.

"Oh, brother."

Frisco had two options open to him.

He could become a babbling idiot from sleep deprivation and hallucinations.

Or he could lock Ms. Helga into his bathroom and call a taxi. He could get the hell out of Dodge City and go somewhere where he could curse when he wanted to, watch *Suntanned Girls from Borneo* when he felt like it and eat all the candy he wanted.

Mostly, he could sleep.

He pulled the card from his cast that Delilah had left him. Lonely Hearts Salon.

Somehow, he had to arrange a jail break.

Flipping the card over, he saw a penciled phone number, and a name: Jerry Wallace, Independent Truck Driver.

Jerry must have meant to give Delilah his phone number, and she'd accidentally put this card inside Frisco's cast.

"Hallelujah!" Frisco yelled. Jerry was the only person Frisco knew who was big enough to help him down the stairs. Plus, he had his own transportation.

And Jerry would understand that Helga, nice as

she might be in one of her previous decades, was no Annabelle. A man could die without the basics of life: Air. Food. Beer.

A beautiful woman.

A pretty baby that slept beside him.

Of course, Annabelle might not have him. She was at a crazy point in her life.

It didn't matter. All he wanted was her bed—and that wasn't too much to ask considering he'd shared his with her.

He dialed the phone.

"Jerry Wallace, independent trucker."

"I need an independent trucker like nobody has ever needed you before. Jerry, it's Frisco Jefferson, and if you come bust me outta here, I'll pay your next month of fuel for that damn rig of yours. It'd have to be a reconnaissance mission of sorts...."

Chapter Thirteen

Deep breath, Annabelle told herself. She hugged Emmie to her a little tighter. The baby was dressed in her prettiest outfit, and she smelled like the sweetest baby soap. If Emmie couldn't charm the socks off a man, they simply couldn't be removed by any means.

Of course, this was Tom. A father wouldn't have to be charmed, would he? It would be a spontaneous, natural bond between father and child?

In Tom's case, maybe not. All he'd been interested in was Dina.

Before Annabelle could muster her courage to step across the street, the door to the Lonely Hearts Salon opened. Her mouth fell open as Tom strolled in, all golden-haired and brightly smiling as always.

"Tom," she said, going weak in the knees from surprise.

"Hello, Annabelle." He approached the carrier

slowly, then said, with more determination than she'd ever seen in him. "Is this my daughter?"

"This is Emmie." Unless he didn't know the difference between a hand puppet and a baby, he knew this was his daughter.

"She doesn't have any hair."

It was probably not best to point out that his was thinning on top, and he was only the south side of forty. Possibly Dina was a bit too vigilant with the scissors. "It will grow one day, Tom."

He looked closer, checking Emmie out. Possibly for defects he couldn't possibly have chromosomed?

Done with his fatherly—or not, as the case certainly had been—perusal, he glanced up at Annabelle. "You're looking well."

She didn't say anything because there was no need. A man who dumped the mother of his child for another woman wasn't interested in what she looked like, before or after. And she certainly wasn't returning the compliment, if that's what he was fishing for.

"I think we should get married," Tom said. "For Emmie's sake."

At that moment, Emmie returned to true form. She let out a bloodcurdling cry that had Tom reeling a good two feet away.

That's one nay vote. "Uh, Tom, could you hand me that diaper bag, please? I need to get her a bottle."

He did, quickly, though he didn't reach in to get the bottle or reach to hold his wailing infant. Frisco would have already had the situation under control, she thought, but that was a useless memory.

A few seconds later, she had Emmie situated with the bottle in her mouth and a pretty bib under her chin. Normally, a burp diaper would have sufficed, but this was her first visit with her father.

"Glad that's over," Tom said. "She's loud, isn't she?"

"She's healthy."

"If she'd been a boy, would she have been as loud?"

Annabelle ground her teeth. "All babies cry," she told him. "When they're hungry, wet or cold."

"So she does that often?"

"Yes, she most certainly does," she affirmed, just so he could have a chance to change his mind about his ridiculous proposal. What had she ever seen in him?

"Back to what I was saying about getting—"

"How's Dina?" she interrupted.

His gaze slid away, a crawling-under-a-rock impression. "We're not seeing each other anymore."

"Really?" She raised her brows. "May I ask why?"

"She just wasn't my type." He glanced down at the baby uncertainly, as she sucked on the bottle.

"It took you eleven months to figure that out? Quick study, huh?"

"I really don't like sarcasm in my women," Tom told her.

Annabelle held back a snort. "I'm not one of your women, Tom."

"No, but you were. Before you got all clingy and marriage-hungry."

She blinked, wondering if she dared bean him with Emmie's bottle. Now that would be sarcasm, or maybe black-humored justice, but then Emmie would be upset and there was no reason to make her cry just because Tom was a louse. "Clingy and marriage-hungry. Well, now that is a reason to dump a woman you've made a baby with. Very valid."

She nodded at him as if he made perfect sense, which he didn't, but he seemed to think he did, and she was still in an incredulous humor-him moment. The mood probably only had a few more seconds before it hit expiration.

He narrowed his eyes. "About getting married, which I think is the right thing to do, considering—"

The door swung open, and the rest of his pompous diatribe was lost. To her amazement—and quite possibly delight, she acknowledged—Frisco limped in, with Jerry's arm supporting him heavily.

The cavalry had arrived. Saved by the bell. And any other cliché she could throw.

She had never been so glad to see a man in all her life. And he looked really *good,* clean-shaven and not shaggy anymore and just overwhelmingly manly in general.

"Frisco!"

"Hey, Annabelle. Don't get up. Emmie needs her bottle. Thanks, Jerry." Obviously worn out and in pain, he propped himself against a rinse bowl. "Nice place."

"What are you doing here?"

"I was going a little stir crazy. Decided to do some traveling. Jerry was coming this way, and I decided to hang a right with him."

"I'm so glad." She smiled at him.

Tom harrumphed.

"Oh, this is Tom. Tom, this is Frisco Joe Jefferson and Jerry Wallace."

The men didn't shake hands. The explosive glares in the room could have sent shrapnel thirty feet.

"I'll feed Emmie," Frisco said. "Come here, little angel," he crooned, taking the baby into his arms.

Annabelle's heart blossomed.

"Who is this, Annabelle?" Tom asked.

"My fiancé," she lied gracefully, with a mental apology to Frisco. But he'd heard about Tom. He wouldn't mind the little fib. She hoped. Frisco puffed up his chest, not looking exhausted anymore, and Annabelle decided he hadn't minded the lie at all.

Tom started laughing. "I don't think so. You can't make me jealous, Annabelle. You'd never fall in love with a broken-down rodeo has-been. Frisco Joe, indeed. Sounds like an old-time bank robber, and you're far too blueblood for that."

"Blueblood?" She turned to stare at him.

He shook his head. "Never mind. Listen, buddy—Frisco Joe—I was just in the middle of proposing to Annabelle. And as that is my daughter, I'd say you're butting in at the wrong time."

"Proposing?" Frisco cocked a brow in that smart-ass manner Annabelle fully recognized. "Where's the candles? The flowers?" He gave Tom a thorough once-over that seemed to shout, What have you done to make her consider a loser like you? "Why aren't you down on one knee?"

"Because I'd get my pants dirty, which isn't sensible at all. And Annabelle's a very sensible girl. If you knew her better, you'd understand that." He looked back at Annabelle, gloating. "Aren't you a sensible girl?"

"Well, hell," Frisco said. "I really didn't want to have to do this, but seeing as how you're making a mess of the whole thing, I'm just going to have to go against my good breeding and cut in line." He handed Emmie to Jerry. The baby made the transition easily, and the truck driver beamed.

Painfully, slowly, Frisco bent his bad leg to the side, gingerly making his way down on one awkward knee. He put his hand over his heart. "Annabelle, belle Anna, you would make me the happiest man on the earth if you'd take me up to your bedroom."

She held back a giggle. Tom's jaw dropped so fast it had rocket propulsion, and Jerry turned his whole body in order to keep from snickering. But she could see his shoulders shaking.

"Come on, Frisco," she said gently. "You need to rest. My bed is perfect for resting."

"Oh, yes, I'm totally exhausted. Just plumb worn out. Completely on my last legs and with one of them in pieces, that's not saying too much," he said dramatically. "See you around, Tom. Thanks, Jerry."

Jerry tipped his cap, a big grin on his face. Annabelle said, "I'll take good care of him, Jerry." Then she helped Frisco from the floor up the stairs, one slow step at a time.

"Thanks for not ratting me out about the fiancé thing," she whispered to him.

"Thanks for not ratting me out about the bedroom thing. I figured I was riding on slim rails with that one."

Annabelle shook her head and tucked her body more firmly under his shoulder. Because he was so tall, she wasn't as much support as she wanted to be. He was gripping the wooden rail tightly as he basically pulled himself up the staircase. "You were perfect. Talk about arriving just in the nick of time."

"I hate for you to leave Emmie in the same room with him." Frisco tried to glance down the stairs but it was too much to twist and stay upright. "I don't think she likes him."

"How could you tell?"

"I don't know. It just seems like she hesitated when you left the room, almost as if she were saying, 'Oh, well, I gotta do what I gotta do, I guess. But I've got Uncle Jerry to protect me at least.' Didn't you notice?"

"Ah, no."

Turning into her room, she helped Frisco to the side of the bed, where he promptly collapsed into it with all his considerable weight and length.

The springs of the bed screamed in protest, and Frisco managed to bounce himself up and down on his back just enough to keep the springs screaming.

"Sounds like we're *really* glad to see each other, doesn't it?" he asked above the squeaking.

Rolling her eyes, she said, "I'm going to get Emmie, so you'd better stop."

He slowed down. "I need another five minutes to be convincing. At least."

"Five...minutes?" She blinked at him.

"You know." He stopped bouncing altogether

and stared at her. "To make it sound like real love-making."

"Oh-h-h. Real lovemaking." She nodded as if that made perfect sense.

His gaze narrowed. "Annabelle—"

Emmie's wail hit a high note. "Oh, my goodness!" Annabelle tore down the stairs. "Let me have her," she said to Tom, who was now holding the baby.

"I didn't do anything!" Tom protested.

Jerry shrugged. "He said anyone could feed a baby and he wanted to give it a go. I thought surely he couldn't mess that up. Unless he pinched her—"

"I did no such thing! She just started crying for no reason!" He glared at the baby as if she'd done it on purpose.

"It's all right. Tom, listen. It's been…interesting, but you'll have to excuse me. I'm real busy right now."

"Okay. I guess. But we need to talk later, Annabelle. That *is* my daughter."

The glance he gave the shrieking baby illustrated his feelings for his daughter. Annabelle guessed those feelings were better expressed, That is my hemorrhoid.

"Jerry, can I do anything for you?"

"No. I've got some local runs to make between here and the panhandle. I'll stop back in and check on you two. Call me when you're ready to get rid of Romeo Joe."

"I thought his name was Frisco Joe," Tom said.

"Not tonight," Jerry told him kindly. "After you, son," he said.

Annabelle sighed, swiftly locking the door. She hurried back up the stairs and walked in the room. Frisco instantly put out his arms. "Bring her here," he commanded. "Plainly this is a woman who knows what's good for her, and she's missed me something fierce!"

"NOW THEN, YOU JUST fall asleep for your Uncle Frisco," he said sweetly. "Watch how I do this," he told Annabelle. "It's like a massage, only at a real reduced level. See how she's putty in my hands."

He put the baby next to him, tucked up against his body. Then he proceeded to touch her neck with two fingers, slowly, down her shoulderblades. Each arm received a delicate caress. He was careful not to press too hard, because women didn't like that. Slowly, gently, soothing. Emmie'd had a hard day—as far as he was concerned he'd gotten here in the nick of time—and nothing felt better to a woman than a foot massage.

But not yet. She had to have the full treatment, because that twerp of a father-come-lately had gotten her all worked up.

After he finished with Emmie, he was going to work Annabelle out of the lather the twerp had put her in, too.

Definitely a foot massage for Annabelle.

"There you go," he whispered to Emmie. "You just let it all go. Breathe in the butterflies. Blow out the bees. I learned that from *Saturday Night Live,* which we may watch together if you're of a mind to stay awake." He kept his voice soft and hypnotic. "Now I'm going to massage these hammy little thighs of yours," he told her, "and you're going to let go of the stress. That's right."

The baby was just about prone now. Her thumb had gone into her mouth, her eyes were barely open. Now for the final phase of the seduction. The feet.

"Trick or treat, I've got your feet, now you go to sleep, good and sweet," he murmured, rubbing her heel. It felt like a little ball between his fingers. Then he moved toward her arch, working it lightly, his fingers finally underneath her toes where he rolled them like early peas between his thumb and forefinger. "Good night, sweetheart," he told her, laying his head down next to hers.

And before he realized it, he'd fallen asleep, too.

ANNABELLE SMILED AT THE big man slumbering next to her child. He'd put both of them to sleep, and nearly her, too, with his mesmerizing voice. Her skin had prickled from imagining Frisco's fingers soothing her the way he was doing Emmie.

The man simply knew his way around her child. Probably women in general, the rat. And he was proud of that fact.

As much as she wanted to join them for a quick nap, she couldn't. She had a proposal to answer, which, caught off-guard, she hadn't been able to think about. There was no time like the present to talk to Tom, while her baby was safe with Frisco. She'd leave him a note, even though she didn't plan on being gone long.

And anyway, she didn't figure she had far to go to find Tom. He'd looked awfully slimy about his Dina-wasn't-my-type story.

She shouldn't have any further to look for him than across the street.

Chapter Fourteen

"Hey, Mimi," said Laredo when she blew through the front door. His non-welcoming tone caught her attention and she halted, counting ten of the Jefferson males sitting in the den watching TV.

Well, now they were watching her.

All ten appeared displeased. "Where's Mason?" she asked, not sure what gave them such disgruntled faces. Maybe Mason was out of town again.

"He's not here right now. Checking some equipment in the barn. But we've darn sure got a bone to pick with you," Tex said.

"What?"

He pointed to the ceiling. "The housekeeper from Hell."

"That's not nice, Tex." Mimi frowned at him. "Mason says she's doing great."

"Because Mason got here after the Lonely Hearts women were here, and he thinks Broomhilda—"

"Helga."

"Precisely. H-e-double-l-g-a." He stared at her to make certain she understood his meaning. Hell-ga. "He thinks Helga is the reason the houses look so nice."

"Isn't it?" She glanced around the room. "It certainly seems tidier in here."

"We don't want it tidy," Fannin told her ominously. "We like living in some fashion of disarray. The remote belongs beside the easy chair. It's always been that way." He gestured to the table where they liked to sit and play cards or dominoes. The table held a pretty, bright finish, instead of dull fingerprints.

"What's wrong with it?"

"We're not allowed to touch it," Ranger said. "How the hell can we play cards if we can't touch the table?"

"It's your table. Do as you like."

"If we do, she'll dust around our elbows while we play. It's quiet warfare between us," Last said. "And I pride myself on being easygoing, but if I have to eat cabbage and sausage one more breakfast, I'm going to have a permanently puckered face."

"Tell Helga what you want to eat," Mimi said reasonably.

"She got upset and went to Mason, telling him we didn't like her cooking. Since he's enamored of the cabbage stuff, he told her that whatever she fixed, we'd eat." Archer was outraged.

Crockett shot her a dirty look. "Of all the tricks you've played on us over the years, Mimi, this one stinks at the lowest level."

"It wasn't a trick! I was trying to be helpful!" She couldn't figure out what they were complaining about, anyway. Didn't they want to have a clean house and hot food?

"It's either me or her," Bandera said.

"You don't even live here, Bandera."

"Yeah, but we eat here and crash here after work to relax. We can't relax like this," Calhoun said. "I've never felt so jumpy in my life. It's like having fleas in my boots."

Navarro shook his head. "Mimi, you've brought good men to their knees."

"Oh, brother. What a bunch of whiners! If you don't like her, have a family council and tell Mason what you've told me. It's ten against one—where's Frisco?"

"It's eleven against one, but Frisco left without casting a vote. He couldn't handle being jailed by Helga the Horrible. She watched him like a hawk, in her version of nursing. But he felt like he was living in a psycho movie, where any minute he was going to open his eyes and find a gray-haired drag queen standing over him, preparing to take a butcher knife to some parts of himself he prizes," Laredo said. "Not that Helga's mean or anything, but she watched him pretty good and it made him crazy, and he got sleep-deprived so that he was starting to hallucinate a bit. Frisco fighting off dream spiders in the night is not much fun to listen to.''

''Poor Frisco! Where did he go?''

Tex shrugged. ''No one knows. He had Jerry come get him when we were all busy. He left a note saying he was going on a long vacation where he could sleep like a baby. Said if he could just get forty-eight hours of undisturbed sleep, he'd be ready to rock.''

She reminded herself that these were grown, if not one-hundred-percent mature, men. They could handle themselves—and Helga—if put to the task. ''Listen, I didn't come over here to listen to y'all bellyache, though I'm sorry you're not happy, but it sounds like your beef is with Mason, since he likes Helga.''

They murmured darkly at that.

''I just wanted for all of you to be the first to know.'' She took a deep breath. ''I'm engaged to be married.''

AT NEARLY THE SAME TIME Mimi made her announcement, Annabelle was making one of her own. ''I'd like to speak with Tom, please,'' she said to the receptionist of the Never Lonely Cut-n-Gurls Salon.

It was true what she'd heard. The chairs *were* red, the lights *were* dim. The infamous slogan *was* on the wall in gold letters. Every mirror had a lavish sign with a woman's name painted on it: Dina, Lola, Sapphire, Ruby, Silk, Emerald, Marvella, Satin and Valentine. Every chair had fresh-cut flowers beside it; the towels were purple. Fragrant candles burned here and there. In the back of the salon, a raised spa bubbled away, big enough for ten people to fit into.

It was all Annabelle could do not to gasp. And no telling what secret pleasure grottos awaited upstairs. No wonder the men brought their business to the salon!

"Tom's not here," said the receptionist, who happened to be Valentine, according to her tight red T-shirt lettered with the name.

"His car is around back," Annabelle said, expecting the excuse. "And either I see him now, or I call the police and let them know you've a lice infestation of biblical proportions. The police and health department will be out on the double, and they may not find lice but from the looks of things, they'll find something else to cite you for."

Valentine snatched up the phone, staring at Annabelle rebelliously. "You're just jealous because Tom left you. And we're putting your salon out of business."

"We don't conduct your kind of business. And as for Tom, I've got a cowboy asleep on my bed, waiting for me, who makes Tom look like the Pillsbury Doughboy with an itty-bitty jelly roll, if you get my drift.'' She snapped her fingers. ''Either you make a call, or I do. Your choice.''

Valentine punched the button. ''Tom's got a visitor,'' she said into the phone. ''No, I don't think *she'll* wait.''

She hung up, her eyes snapping sparks at Annabelle. Examining her long fingernails, she said nonchalantly, ''How's the baby?'' in the tone of someone who thought babies were living hell.

''Going to grow up to be a lady,'' Annabelle shot back. ''You'll have to look that word up in a dictionary. Tom, thanks for sparing me a moment of your time,'' she said, as he came down the stairs, his light hair awry and his trousers unzipped, though buttoned.

Dina followed behind him a second later, bearing a furious expression and no lipstick, since Tom had it on his fly. Note to self—red lipstick shows bigtime on khakis.

Thank heavens Frisco preferred blue jeans, onelegged as they were right now due to his cast. Red wouldn't be quite as startling on denim—although as Tom had said, she was a sensible girl. She knew where to leave her lipstick, and it wouldn't be on the fabric.

''What happened to you not wanting to get your trousers dirty proposing?''

''Huh?'' he asked, clearly hoping to play dumb.

Well, that wasn't too hard for him. ''I've thought

over your marriage proposal," she said to Tom, "and I—"

"Marriage proposal?" Dina demanded.

Tom's guilty expression gave away the wrong answer. Dina slapped the guilt and maybe two layers of skin clean off his face. "You slimy turd!" she screamed.

"Oh, that was painful," Annabelle said sympathetically, silently applauding Dina. Now Tom's cheek matched his crotch, and it was all good in her book. "I can't accept the proposal, of course. But my lawyer will be contacting you to arrange the paperwork for visitation, should you want it, and, of course, for child support payments."

"Child support payments!" he howled. "You've got a lot more money than I have, Annabelle. Millions! I'm going to sue you for...palimony or something! I have rights in this, too."

"How do you know about my financial situation?" She hadn't expected him to want to pay— that had been a bonus jab for fun—but she was curious as to why he thought he deserved palimony. Ridiculous, since no court would consider such a stupid claim, but all the same, she wanted to know.

"You're Annabelle Turnberry of Turnberry Wines, and you just came into your father's entire fortune and estates." He shook his finger at her. "I don't have to pay you a dime."

"You're not paying me," she said quietly. "You're

living up to your responsibility by seeing to your daughter's future. If you choose not to do that, I'm certain that my lawyer could work out a deal with you. No child support, no visitation."

He glared at her. "I don't want to see her anyway."

For Emmie's sake, her heart broke, but she'd expected no less. She'd been prepared. The truth was, she'd fallen for Tom when she was in pain from her father's death. She'd thought he was someone he wasn't, but her innocence was spent. She wouldn't make that mistake again.

Emmie had her, and that was enough.

"I'm sorry to hear that, Tom. I'll have my lawyers send you the paperwork—to this address, I guess?"

"Hell, no!" Dina shrieked. "You get out of here, you two-timing, lying, bellycrawling shyster! And you'd better pay me the thousand dollars you borrowed, or...or—" She glanced at Annabelle for inspiration. "Or you'll be hearing from *my* lawyer!"

He stared at both of them, his mouth gaping open.

"Tom, your fly is open," Annabelle said.

MASON SHOOK HIS HEAD like a big bear, trying to clear it from what Laredo had just said. "Mimi's engaged? Who would marry her? I didn't even know she was dating anyone."

He was babbling. He certainly didn't want to hear

any more than he just had. "Maybe you heard wrong."

"No, she came over to tell us first, she said. And she was wearing a huge rock, though none of us recovered fast enough to ask who'd given it to her."

"Maybe it's a fake," Mason said.

Laredo shrugged. "I doubt it. It sure was catching the light. Anyway, why would she fake having an engagement ring?"

"Fake engagement," Mason clarified, the last hope available to him sounding odd even to his ears. "Don't think she would. She seemed very serious. Like I've never seen her this serious."

Mimi had clearly been swept off her feet by the Ferrari city dude. "Well," he said slowly, "I wish her all the best. Guess I'll get to meet him sooner or later."

"Probably not until the wedding. And after that, she's moving to Houston with him. At least that's what Sheriff Cannady said."

"Houston!" Mason thought that sounded highly unlikely. "Mimi doesn't belong in Houston."

"Well, she's been here all her life. I think she's probably ready to move on. Raise her own family and all. She'll be a good mom, although I have a hard time seeing her driving a van in car pools and dragging snacks to soccer games. Sitting on the sidelines with the cheerleaders and doing booster club stuff. Actually, I don't have a problem seeing that at all," Laredo said thoughtfully. "Mimi will do awesome. She's got all that energy she's never known what to do with."

"Mimi...raise a family?" Mason's heart slid somewhere below his boots, right into the very ground he stood on. He couldn't imagine her pregnant, had never thought of her in that manner. "What for? I mean, why would she do that?"

Laredo smirked at him. "Because everybody who doesn't live at the Malfunction Junction usually wants one, bro."

"I suppose." He didn't. He'd thought she felt the same way. For some reason, he felt a bit betrayed. "I never knew she wanted children."

"Don't worry about it." Laredo slapped him on the back. "You'll make a great uncle."

DELILAH HUNG UP HER cell phone with a smile. "Jerry said he dropped Frisco Joe off in town to visit Annabelle," she told her staff. She was happy about that, because she had a funny feeling those two had something to talk about and maybe a little more, but she had something sad to tell the rest of her girls: Beatrice, Carly, Daisy, Dixie, Gretchen, Hannah, Jessica, Julie, Katy, Kiki, Lily, Marnie, Remy, Shasta, Tisha, Velvet and Violet.

She was going to miss them.

"There's something I have to tell you all. This week has been a vacation of sorts, or at least that's what I told you. Actually, it was my last chance to be part of a big family. I'm going to have to cut back, girls," she said softly. "I'm sorry, because you are all like daughters to me. Unfortunately, I'm not making what I was at the salon, and now I'm barely covering the rent."

The women sitting and drinking coffee with her in the highway-side coffee shop stared at her with trepidation.

"Cut back?" Katy Goodnight asked. "How much?"

"I'm going to have to reduce my staff by fifty percent."

A gasp of dismay met that announcement.

"I couldn't feel worse about this. But since my sister opened her salon across the street, my life has changed in many ways, and I don't think I have to tell you that."

Kiki nodded. "We understand, Delilah. You took most of us in when we had no place else to go, and we've been grateful for that. When will you tell us who has to go?"

"I'd as soon know now," Shasta said.

Delilah nodded. "Fair enough. Was anyone planning on turning in their notice to me any time soon?"

No one spoke up. She hadn't expected them to. They'd been a family for a while. Most of these women had no place else to go. Or they chose not to. Sighing, she tore paper strips off the place mat. "I've thought about this every which-a-way. I could go on a seniority basis. I could go on a most-earned basis. None of these ways strikes me as particularly fair, because I love all of you, and that's not a business emotion. They say not to mix business and pleasure, but you girls have been my pleasure, and without you, I wouldn't have had a business. So. I'm going to draw names."

Her heart bleeding, she wrote each name on a paper. Every stroke of the pen made her hand shake more. She didn't think she'd be able to write the last name; the pen felt as heavy as an executioner's blade. "I'm so sorry," she whispered.

"It's all right," Kiki said. "We know you did your best, Delilah. We all did."

Delilah nodded, taking a deep gulping breath. She put the papers all together in a pile she'd rather have burned than use for its intended purpose and covered it with her hands, prayer-like, with her eyes closed. "Ready?"

"As we'll ever be," Shasta said.

"All right." Behind closed eyes, she held back tears. Her business, these women, were all she'd ever had in her life that gave her pleasure. These were her sisters the way Marvella never would be; these were the daughters she would never have; these were the friends who shared her happiness and tears.

These girls were pieces of her soul.

"Annabelle," she said, reading the first piece of paper she pulled from underneath her other hand. The other girls gasped and some began to sob. Annabelle had a baby and a broken heart. It would kill her to tell her she had to go.

"Beatrice, Gretchen, Jessica, Lily, Marnie, Tisha, Velvet, Violet," she read, pulling names as fast as she could to get it over with before she broke down and cried.

"Carly, Daisy, Dixie, Hannah, Julie, Katy, Kiki, Remy, and Shasta remain employed at the Lonely Hearts Salon. Now, if anything should change, anything at all, I—I—" She couldn't hold back any longer. Putting her head down on the Formica table in the roadside restaurant, she cried as she'd never cried in her whole life.

Except maybe when Marvella had accused Delilah of stealing her husband. That had been the knife driven into her heart.

The wound had never healed, and today, it started bleeding all over again.

Chapter Fifteen

It was near evening when Frisco awakened—evening of the next night. "I think the winter weather is making you and Emmie hibernate," she told him.

"Have you been in this bed?" he demanded.

"Yes, and Emmie's been up for feeding and playtime. You never moved."

"Jeez. I'm so sorry." He sat up, running his hand through his hair so that it stood straight up.

"I think you were very tired," she said with a smile.

"I was more tired than I've ever been in my life. Did I tell you about Helga, the hellish housekeeper Mimi hired?"

She shook her head, jealous already, especially if she was the cause of Frisco not getting any sleep. Although hellish didn't sound like he was that crazy about her.

"She nearly drove me out of my skull. Imagine having someone staring at you twenty-four-seven, waiting for you to move, trying to give you pills, cleaning your room—you'd think a seventy-year-old woman would want to sit down occasionally, wouldn't you?''

"Seventy." Annabelle nodded as if she'd automatically known that, but warmed to the core that Mimi hadn't hired some sweet young thing. "Maybe she's over-compensating. She could really need the job."

"I don't know. I just knew I had to get out of there or I was going to jump out my window. Hope you don't mind me running to you. But this was the only place I knew where there'd be some serious sleeping going on. Emmie sure does like her snooze time. And so does her Uncle Frisco," he said, looking down at the baby who was too asleep to care about Uncle Frisco at the moment.

"Jumping out your window would be bad with your busted leg," Annabelle reminded him.

"Don't I know it. Jerry is a man of principle, honor, duty and integrity, you know it. And any other complimentary word you can think of."

"That about covered it," she said. "Can I get you something to eat?"

"My treat. What's in this town?"

"Whatever you want. Prepared questionably."

"What's the local specialty? That can be delivered? No cabbage, though."

She shook her head. "I hate cabbage."

"Wait a minute. I want to see what's across the street." He staggered to his feet, hopping over to the window. Staring out at the Never Lonely Cut-n-Gurls Salon, he whistled. "Bet I know what they cook over there. Look at those T-shirts walking in, would you?"

She went behind him and snapped the blinds down. "T-shirts are cheap."

"Uh, yes. Yes, you're right about that. A dime a dozen." He gave her the most mischievous grin she'd ever seen on a man. "I just wanted you close to me, Annabelle. Gotcha." He reached out and snaked an arm around her before she could protest, pulling her tight against him. "Now, that's worth a two-hour drive and an Italian dinner, complete with candles. What do you think?"

"That I love spaghetti," she said, loving the feel of him holding her in their first real embrace. "It might be akin to sauerkraut in visual effects, though."

"No. Trust me, they are not even distant cousins. I missed your cooking, Annabelle."

"You did not. I'm not a good cook."

"But you tried hard. That matters." He looked at her, his eyes gleaming in the moonlight streaming in from behind the blinds. "In fact, I'm beginning to think just about everything about you matters."

She held her breath, surprised. So he kissed her, and she didn't move anything except her lips, until her body took over her fears and she slid her arms around his neck, pulling him close the way he'd done her.

This time, there was nothing about their kiss that was friendly. It was hot and hungry and passionate.

"This is just friends," she gasped. "Right?"

He propped her against him so that he bore her weight as he leaned against the wall, and she leaned into him, willing to move with him.

"What else would it be?" he asked between searching kisses.

"Nothing that I can think of." Her hands moved across his chest, back over his shoulders to slide under his Western shirt. "Except maybe best friends. You shouldn't sleep in all your clothes."

"The very best of best friends. I had to sleep in all my clothes. We're alone together in this big salon. You might get wild ideas about my cowboy body."

He nipped at her earlobe, and she tilted back her head, sighing. "I never had wild ideas before. I think I like it."

A groan escaped him as her hands wandered. "I saw you going into the competition's den over there."

She leaned her head again to look at him. "You couldn't have. You were asleep."

"I have acute hearing. The sound of unfamiliar

doors opening and closing had me peg-legging to the window.''

She smiled at him, pulling his face down so that she could nuzzle his chin. ''I'm sorry. If I'd known that, I would have told you.''

''Not that it really matters, because we're just best friends, but—''

''The change in Tom was due to discovering that I had money of my own.''

''I should whip his hide.''

She shook her head and ran her hands around his waist. ''Dina already did.''

''Dina? Good woman.''

''Probably not, but it was okay by me if she did the dirty work. So, you already knew who my family was?''

''A little birdie told me. But that's not why I'm here.''

She laughed low and husky, moving her hands from his waist down inside the back of his jeans. ''I didn't think so.''

''I just think we should get that straight. I'd rather cut off one of my appendages than be a kept man, and even if we didn't need to get that drastic, I'm not hurting financially.''

''I know.'' She kissed his chin. ''You wanted to shack up with me so you could sleep.''

''Yes, but I'm wild-eyed and bushy-tailed now.''

She slid her hands from the back of his jeans to the front. "Something like that."

"Annabelle, honey, you're heaping flames onto an already raging fire."

Her gaze went to his eyes. "I want to be so sophisticated about this, Frisco, but it's just not in me."

"I know." He kissed her forehead.

"Um, remember what you said about needing five minutes of squeaking my springs to give Tom the impression that we were making love properly?"

"Yes." His eyes were patient, waiting.

"And you know what I told you about the sign painted on the wall across the street that said Save A Horse; Ride A Cowboy?"

"Yes, babe."

"Cowboys try to stay on for eight seconds, right?"

"Mm. If they want to win."

"My experience at the rodeo ended before the bell. Or the buzzer, or the gong, or whatever it is that—"

"Annabelle." He pulled back to look into her eyes. "Honey, you're not saying what I think you're saying, are you?"

"It was my first and only time," she said miserably.

"Whew." He glanced from her to Emmie. "You must be one fertile lady. Holy Christmas, and we've got three sets of twins amongst my siblings alone. You could be the gift that keeps on giving.''

She tried to smile.

''So…no sweethearts before Him-Who-Had-No-Staying-Power?''

''No. My father had Alzheimer's for ten years. I was his sole caretaker because I wanted it that way. I don't regret it for a minute. But it left me without a social life, the usual flings and break-ups and drama that are part of normal learning. And then, when my father passed away, I was shattered,'' she said quietly. ''I think I just wanted someone to care for me for a change. You can see why I don't want any more children. At least not right now.''

He hugged her to him, close and sheltering. ''I completely understand. I don't want any except Emmie. I mean, you know what I mean. Best friends and all that. Uncle Frisco.''

Her blush felt like it was all over her body. ''I was afraid you'd be disappointed.''

''Because you don't want more children?'' At her nod, he said, ''Annabelle, you don't even begin to know how relieved I am. Count the brothers around my house and tell me we need more bodies to fall over.''

She lowered her gaze. ''And you're not disappointed about…the other?''

''The other what?''

''My lack of experience in pleasing a man?''

He laughed out loud. "Annabelle, you please *this* man. As far as I can see, I'm getting the best of all worlds here. I get a sexy lady, a best friend and a virgin all wrapped up in one, plus a sweet baby to hold that's mine in spirit. Where am I lacking?"

"Frisco, you see me in a light I've never seen myself," she said shyly.

"Well, that's because I can see in the dark," he said confidently. "And right now I'm going to see you, and feel you, and hold you, and take you. And before the night is over, you're going to know what it means to be really loved. I've got plenty of those things you found in my drawer—"

"I remember. Striped with fluorescent colors," she said. "Stars and an interesting device on the tip for maximum pleasure."

"And I can hang on well past the bell, Annabelle. I would never let you down."

"Oh, my gosh," she said on a moan, as he opened her shirt and suckled her breasts.

Then he kissed her lips before moving back to lick each nipple. "Tonight, we're going to test just how sound Emmie can sleep. Because I won't have done my job unless they hear you come across the street. Can you count to eight, Annabelle?" he murmured against her skin.

"Yes," she whispered, her whole body beginning to tremble at the possessive, meaningful promise behind Frisco's words.

"Then let's see about saving some horses."

He slid her blouse to the floor.

THE ONLY THING THAT could move Annabelle to leave her bed the next morning was Emmie urgently requesting a feeding time.

"I'll get her," Frisco said, kissing Annabelle on the lips before he swung his bad leg to the side of the bed. "Come here, little princess. Let's me and you go hunt big game bah-bah. Where's the kitchen, pretty mama?"

Annabelle practically cackled into her pillow, loving Frisco's ridiculous chit-chat with her daughter and his silliness in general. "At the end of the hall is a mini-fridge and microwave. Eight," she said on a groan. "I stopped counting, but I'm pretty sure it was eight." Frisco had loved her until she screamed, laughed, cried and sometimes was torn between which she should do. It was the most amazing thing that had ever happened to her.

And he still got up to feed her baby. "I don't know, Frisco. If I'd met you first, I'm sure I would have fallen in love with you. I never would have even seen another man," she muttered facedown in the pillow.

"What's that?" he said, coming back into the room with a bottle and Emmie.

"Nothing. I was just saying how glad I am that we're best friends."

"What'd I tell you. There's men who know how to be friends to a woman, and then there's men who give other men a lazy reputation. The few of us who know what we're about become legends."

She rolled over, laughing at him. "It's been a while for you, too, huh?"

"At least a year," he replied, sheepish as he sat down. "But it wasn't for lack of willing victims."

"What was it then?" She sat up against the pillows, pulled the sheet up over her breasts and stared at him.

"I'm discriminating. Only the best." He jerked the sheet to her waist with the hand that wasn't holding Emmie's bottle. "That's what I like to see in the morning. Your navel," he teased.

She blushed as her nipples tightened from the brisk temperature in the room—and his very interested perusal. He was no more looking at her navel than she was looking at his, though it was attractive as a man's navel went. Trying to ease the sheet back up when he wasn't looking was futile—he held it in a knot.

"Don't deprive a man of one of the few joys in his life. Especially take pity on me because of my broken leg. I need a visual focus while I feed this child for you."

"It's hard," she protested.

"It most definitely is." He leered at her.

"I've never been a man's visual focus. I've never

been this naked around a man.'' He was practically eating her alive with his eyes. ''I've got to take a shower.'' She leapt out of bed before he could grab her ankle, though he tried. ''Frisco, I couldn't make love again even if I wanted to. Trust me.''

To her surprise, not three minutes later, he joined her in the shower, with Emmie, cast wrapped.

''I'm not going to make love to you in the shower—not today, anyway,'' he teased. ''But this is a moment I can't pass up.'' He held Emmie against his chest, and Annabelle against Emmie's back and against his shoulder, and the three of them stood under the warm spray, enjoying the feel of each other. Not seductive. Just close.

Necessary.

It felt like a real family: a mother, a father, a baby. All happy. She loved it.

She was falling in love with Frisco Joe Jefferson.

In fact, she was long past falling.

Chapter Sixteen

An hour later, as Annabelle and Frisco sat in the kitchen eating breakfast, pounding on the downstairs door sent Annabelle jumping to her feet. "I'll go see who it is."

"Tom, most likely."

"I don't think so. He'd call at this point, since he knows you're here."

"Or slither under the door. A snake could slither under the door, right?" He kissed Emmie's forehead while the infant gazed up at him adoringly. "I shouldn't talk badly about your father," he told her. "I should teach you to love your mother and father. Your mother, that's a piece of cake. Your father is a whole other matter in spiritual charity."

"Frisco," Annabelle said on a laugh. "I'll be right back."

Hurrying to the door, she pondered how much her life had changed—for the better. She was no longer sad; she no longer mourned her father. She would always miss him, of course, but now she felt as if she could move on and live a happy life. She and Emmie.

It was all turning out so much better than she had ever dreamed—thanks to the man who'd taught her everything about herself she'd needed to know.

Jerry's red nose and cheery blue eyes were peeking in the glass pane. She opened the door, motioning for him to come inside. "Hello!" Giving him a big hug, she said, "It's a cold wind that blew you back here, Jerry. Can I get you some coffee?"

"I'd accept that offer."

"Great. Frisco, Jerry's here!"

The two of them went into the kitchen, and Frisco stood to shake Jerry's hand. "Got your haul taken care of?"

"That I did," Jerry said, seating himself. "Thought I'd stop here on my way and see if you wanted a ride back to Union Junction."

Her hand froze over the coffee pot. It made perfect sense that Frisco would return with Jerry. He couldn't stay here forever.

"Did I ever tell you that you look like Santa Claus?" Frisco asked.

"Actually, yes, you did." Jerry's eyes twinkled at him. "It's a compliment to me and my red Kenworth sleigh, hauling goodies. 'Course, last time you called me Santa, you'd just busted your leg and were jabbering like mad."

Frisco frowned. "I don't remember."

Annabelle set coffee in front of the two men. "Here you go," she said, taking Emmie from Frisco. "I'll hold her so you can get your things."

"I didn't say I was going, did I? Did I say I was leaving?"

He looked at her, and Annabelle smiled. "It's okay. I'll be all right now, Frisco."

Hesitating, he looked at her and then the baby. And then her again. "Annabelle, I—"

They were just friends. She didn't want more from him than that because it wasn't right to expect more. Though Tom had called her marriage-hungry and clingy, that had been him making himself feel better. She didn't want Frisco to think he had to prop her up forever.

And besides, what were they going to do? Stay here and make love until they got sick of each other? Follow him to Union Junction and be his house-keeper? That wasn't the way she wanted Emmie raised. She owed it to her daughter to set a stable, loving example of motherhood. "It's for the best," Annabelle said.

"I guess you're right. I'll get my things and join you in a moment, Jerry."

"Take your time. Lemme hold that little toot. You go say goodbye."

Handing the baby over, she went up the stairs with a heavy heart. It would be a difficult goodbye, but she was getting used to those. "Frisco," she said, entering her room, "thank you for coming to see me. And Emmie."

He shook his head at her. "You sound like we'll never see each other again. I kind of hear it in your voice. You know, Delilah says you don't stick in one place for long."

"Well, I didn't. But I'm going to now. I owe it to Emmie."

"Oh." He smiled at her. "You're a good mother, Annabelle." And then he hugged her, and Annabelle hugged him back, with tears in her eyes she wouldn't let him see. "Goodbye, Frisco."

"Bye." He kissed her, a sweet goodbye kiss, not on the cheek like friends but on the lips like best friends and a bit more. "Miss me a little, okay?"

"I will."

Nodding, he went down the stairs. She followed, taking Emmie from Jerry.

"I'll see you soon, no doubt," Jerry said. "Now that I know where the salon is, I might as well get my hair trimmed here. On my way through."

"Me, too," Frisco said.

Annabelle nodded, not saying a word.

"Bye, gal. You mind yourself," Jerry said.

Frisco kissed Emmie on the forehead. "And you mind yourself, sweetie. Mind your mother."

They walked out, waving in the cold winter air.

Annabelle waved back, then closed the door and locked it.

The salon seemed dark and silent without them. She'd never noticed the lack of light and laughter before.

The sisterhood was the best part of the salon. She'd miss it, but she was strong enough now to leave the sisterhood and forge ahead. She had a responsibility to Emmie—and to herself. "Come on, sweetie," she said. "Let's go pack up. It's time to go home."

FRISCO KNEW THE MINUTE he stepped out of the salon that he was making a mistake. The feeling followed him from Lonely Hearts Station halfway to Union Junction.

What had that friends stuff been all about? Maybe he still had some screws knocked loose from when he broke his leg, because he sure didn't feel "friendly" about Annabelle.

It had seemed like the wise, self-preserving description of the relationship at the time. Mainly because he hadn't wanted to rush her.

But damn it, he felt like he'd just walked out on the best thing he'd ever had.

Best friends, his foot. He sounded like he'd had his head slammed in a psych text book and forgot to have feelings of his own. He should have swept her off her feet. Maybe she wasn't quite ready for a long-term relationship, but he had a big broom. He could sweep her so that she liked it.

"Something on your mind, friend?" Jerry asked.

"Not really. Yes, actually. I'm wishing I hadn't left without saying something to Annabelle."

"I got a cell phone."

"Thanks, no, I've got one, too." He scratched his head. "What I want to say can't be said on a cell phone. I'd have to be holding her in my arms."

"Kenworth hanging a U-ee," Jerry said. "It's gonna be wide and short, so hang on."

"Wide and short?" Frisco asked with some alarm. "What are you doing?"

Jerry pulled to the left side of the highway, where there was a spot to turn around. "We're going back to Lonely Hearts Station."

"You don't have to take me back."

"How else you going to get there with a busted spoke?"

"I don't know."

"And didn't you say it had to be said in person?" He'd poked fun at Tom for not putting enough effort into what he was saying to Annabelle. "Yes, it does."

"Then back we go."

"Jerry, you are more than a friend to me."

"Nah, at this moment, I'm tacking on freight charges for you and your cast. I'm adding it to the month's worth of fuel you promised to pay." But he chuckled, and Frisco knew the big trucker had a soft spot for a good love story.

"You're great to help me out."

"I'm a trucker. I like the road, and it likes me. Sit back, close your eyes and compose your speech. I want it to be worth it when we get there."

Frisco grinned, leaning his head back and closing his eyes. Finally, he'd found a woman he cared enough about to hang a U-ee for.

THE LONELY HEARTS SALON was dark by the time Jerry pulled into a parking space on the town square. "Did she have a light on before?"

Frisco frowned. "Seemed like she had some lights on."

With a bad feeling inside his suddenly racing heart, Frisco jumped down from truck. Going to the door, he pounded, all the while peering through the glass, trying to see inside.

"I'll try to raise her on the cell phone," Jerry called from the truck cab.

After five minutes, when Frisco knew she wasn't in the bathroom, and she wasn't busy with the baby, and she wasn't going to open the door, a voice at his elbow made him nearly jump out of his boots.

"She's gone," a petite redhead said.

"Gone?"

"Left town. Went back home."

"How do you know?"

The redhead gave him a saucy once-over. Frisco realized she was wearing a Never Lonely glittered T-shirt. She batted long eyelashes at him coyly. If he hadn't been in love—yes, damn it, in love—he might have been interested in the game she was offering. As it was, he just wanted her to spill info.

"My name's Valentine," she said. "I work over there."

"I got that. Why would you know what Annabelle was doing?"

"Because she came over and left a message for Tom with me. Tom used to see Dina, until she found out he was trying to snake her with Annabelle." Valentine's tone was outraged. "The two-timing skunk."

"Ah, yeah." Valentine had twisted logic, but her shirt was cut short enough to show her midriff, and even in winter, he had to think a woman like her could get cold enough to stop thinking straight. "So, can you share the message with me? That she left for Tom."

"I could, cowboy, if you were nice to me."

He gulped. "How nice do I have to be?"

"Come into our salon," she said, in the voice of the spider luring the fly. "We've been looking for customers all day."

On another day, such an offer might have been worthy. Today, he just wanted to track Annabelle. "Listen, I'm in a big hurry, so maybe…would you be interested in a crisp Ben Franklin?'' He took out the money Annabelle would never take back from him and held it up.

Valentine snatched it like it might blow away any second. "She went home to the family winery. With Emmie. She told Tom that she was having her lawyer send papers to arrange for sole custody, there was no money involved for him and if he messed with her, she'd make certain the bank foreclosed on that fancy car he recently bought.''

"Well, I'm sure he talked a good game. Now, listen to me, Valentine, because this is important. Do you know where the family winery is located?''

"No. I don't drink wine,'' she said with a sniff. "Only sexy drinks.''

"Sexy drinks?''

"You know. The kind you have to shake.'' She leaned against his arm, bouncing a little for illumination.

"Er, thank you for all your help. It's been great talking to you,'' he said, being nice as he backed away in case he ever needed to use her for an info source again. "Goodbye!'' Jumping into Jerry's truck, he slammed the door and locked it. "Gee whiz!''

He could hear Jerry sniggering into his sleeve. "What are you laughing about?''

"That little gal didn't care about your broken leg.

She was gonna crawl right up you and eat you alive.''

"Yeah, well, she'll have to go hungry a while longer. No wonder Delilah's having trouble keeping clientele.''

Jerry sobered instantly. "Damn shame, that.''

It *was* a shame because Delilah was a nice lady trying to do right for women who had no other place to go. He sighed. "All right. Do you know where Annabelle's family home was?''

"Somewhere in central Texas.''

This was harder than he'd anticipated. Trust Annabelle to throw up a challenge he couldn't meet by himself. He couldn't drive there with a broken leg, he couldn't fly because he didn't think he could get his leg to fit in the tiny space in front of an airline seat.

"I need to go home and think about this,'' he said. "Maybe the best thing for me to do is give Annabelle some space.'' His heart had sunk the instant Valentine had told him Annabelle was gone. She'd wasted no time lighting out of Lonely Hearts Station after he'd gone.

"I'm sorry you wasted a trip on me, Jerry,'' he told his friend. "While my first inclination was to go after her, my second is that...she has my number if she wants to call me. She knows where I live.''

"If you say so.'' Jerry looked as confused as he

did. "I wouldn't have thought she'd light out that fast. But I told you what Delilah said—"

"I know. I know. Annabelle's a rolling stone." And he wasn't so sure she hadn't just rolled right over him. Dang. "If you don't mind taking me home, I'd surely appreciate it," Frisco said.

Home to Helga the Horrible.

H-e-double hockey sticks-g-a.

He was going to take up window-jumping.

Chapter Seventeen

"This place sucks!" Last told Tex and Laredo two weeks later. "I'm praying for March and some good stiff winds to blow out the bad aura around this joint."

"It's the same as it's always been at the Malfunction Junction," Laredo said. "Quit yer bitching."

"It's not," Last insisted. "Mason doesn't say a word. I think he's forgotten what his lips are for. And I won't even discuss Frisco. He's forgotten what his heart is for, and he sold his soul to Oscar the Grouch."

"He'll look good in green fur," Tex said without much sympathy.

"Speaking of looking good in fur, did you see the one Mimi had on the other day? I realize it was simulated, but it wasn't cheap-simulated. She said her fiancé gave it to her as an engagement gift!"

Last's voice clearly communicated his disbelief. Laredo cocked a brow at him. "So?"

"Well, it's Mimi we're talking about. What's she gonna do with a full-length fur? Feed her goat?"

"It's really none of our business," Tex told him sourly.

"Well, don't act like you're not depressed as hell."

Tex pounded his hand on the table, which brought Helga running with a cloth. They all waited politely until she was done wiping up the fist print, but as soon as she left the room, Last leaned forward to whisper urgently, "Everything has gone cockeyed around here and you know it. We've got to *do* something!"

Laredo was of half a mind to agree, but he'd been busy hatching his plan to hit the road. All he had on his mind was a merciful escape. "Talk to Ranger."

"Ranger isn't going to do anything. He's been so buggy over his military books he pays me no mind."

"There's half a dozen more of us. Go bother them."

Last drew himself up. "If you don't care, why should I? If no one cares, then fine. You can all just steep in your misery."

"What do you want us to do? Tell Mimi that

Mason misses his playmate? Tie Helga up and ship her back to Europe? Find Frisco a woman?''

"That was the original plan, if you recall. We said a woman would take care of his bad temper. And it did.''

"For a while,'' Tex agreed. "Now he's blacker than night. I think it had the adverse effect.''

Last shook his head. "He's in love, stupids.''

"What does that have to do with us?'' Laredo wanted to know.

"You could offer to help him,'' Last suggested.

"It's really, really bad to try to help other people's love lives. Haven't we gotten burned on that one?''

"Isn't doing something better than nothing?'' Last asked.

"No,'' Tex and Laredo said in unison.

"Well, fine.'' Last backed away from the table. "The problem here is, no one remembers that this used to be a happy home.''

"Last, listen. You were the baby. You had life easier than the rest of us. Of course you remember it with lollipop-colored vision,'' Laredo told him.

Tex snickered and looked out the window.

"Hey, that's not true. Mom was a good mom.''

His brothers didn't say a word.

"You know it's true. And Dad was crazy about her. When she passed away, he lost all his heart to go on without her. Can't you see that's happening to Frisco?''

Laredo rolled his eyes, but he was beginning to realize that Last was serious. He was a serious pain in the keister, one that wasn't going to be relieved until he got what he wanted.

And maybe, partially, he had the story right.

"You're so sensitive," he told his youngest brother. "What the hell do you want from us?"

"I think you should offer to drive Frisco to find Annabelle."

Laredo raised his brows. "How do you know he'd go?"

"I don't think he would, willingly."

"So we kidnap him and force him to be happy with Annabelle? And you say I've got problems," Tex griped.

"He doesn't know how to win Annabelle. He's afraid she won't have him. But I say, he who chickens out, never wins his feathers."

Laredo snorted. "After we make this ridiculous offer to chauffeur our brother, and he eats our head, will you shut up and leave us alone about it? Or go write a romance novel in the privacy of your own room?"

"I promise I will."

"All right. If this is what it takes to get you to go bother someone else, I'm on my feet." Laredo looked at Tex. "Are you going with me? Two of us should be able to subdue Frisco."

Tex grinned. "What the hell."

Slowly, the three of them ascended the staircase. Laredo tapped on Frisco's door.

"Go away," he called impatiently.

"Frisco, can we talk to you a minute?" Laredo called.

The door opened. "Is Helga nearby?"

"No," Tex said looking over his shoulder.

"Come in, then. Hurry!"

The three brothers jumped into the room. Frisco slammed the door and locked it. "I've started leaving by the window when I want to get away. Just like the old days."

"Really? You're going to break your other leg," Laredo said, peering out the window. "Drain pipe or sheets?"

"I reinforced the drain pipe and keep a tall ladder hidden behind the crape myrtles down there."

"Good thinking. Hey, me and Tex were thinking about taking a drive. Wanna go with?"

"Where you headed?" Frisco asked, perking up.

"Texas wine country," Tex said nonchalantly.

"Oh. No, I think I'd better stay here."

"Don't be such a coward, Frisco. What's happened to you?" Laredo demanded. "You used to be so hellfire and brimstone but now you're too quiet.

I liked you better the other way. At least you had *cojones*."

Frisco was silent for a moment. "Maybe."

"Why are you taking it so personal, bro?" Tex asked. "You knew she had a life of her own."

"Yeah, but that doesn't mean I thought she'd leave me out of it. I mean, I shared my life with her."

"You did? I find that hard to believe," Laredo told him.

"Well, I shared my bed, and my room, and—you know, she didn't say goodbye. I mean, that brings up all kinds of insecurities."

"Yours, apparently. Call her, then. Ask if she would like to see you."

Frisco brightened. "I could do that. I could call her."

"Sure. You just put your finger on the phone and push some buttons. No problem." Tex handed him the phone.

"Um. Okay." He held the phone as it if were ticking. Then he took a deep breath and dialed Information. "Annabelle Turnberry, please, in Austin or the suburbs," he guessed. Tex shrugged, Laredo nodded and Last scratched his head.

"That number is unlisted, sir. Can I try another number for you?"

"No. I don't think so. Thanks anyway." He hung

up and glared at his brothers. "That was a really dumb idea."

"Why didn't you ask for Turnberry Wines?" Last asked.

Frisco shook his head. "I can't just call her, guys. It's not the way I feel. A phone call is for friends."

Laredo sighed. "I'll get my truck keys. Last, pack us a cooler."

Frisco limped to grab his already-packed duffle. "Thanks. I really appreciate this."

"Hey! Why are you already packed?" Tex demanded.

"Because I was about to succumb to paying taxi fare all the way to the Turnberry Winery." He grinned at his brothers. "But since you've graciously offered, I'd much rather take up the back seat of the double cab."

"Great," Laredo grumbled.

"You guys are the best brothers."

"Great," Tex echoed. "Last, we're going to tie you up and leave you for the roadside pick-up if you open your mouth between here and Austin!"

ANNABELLE WALKED UPSTAIRS to her father's study, entering on quiet feet. It had been nearly a year since she'd been back in their home. The housekeeper and groundskeeper had done a nice job of maintaining it.

That was a comfort to her.

The house was lined in dark wood with delicate floral rugs, elegant hanging chandeliers. In every room, she could hear the laughter of happier times.

She could also feel the moments Alzheimer's had stolen from their lives. She closed the door of the study.

"Well, Dad," she said out loud. "I miss you more than I knew I could miss someone. It's really, really difficult." Swallowing hard, she sat down in the leather chair behind his desk. Here she'd played under his feet as a child, while he conducted business calls; here she'd read many a book as a teenager, while her father met business associates. As a young woman, she had been an active hostess for her father and had discovered the business aspects of the winery came easily to her.

"I've really let you down, Dad," she whispered. "You said I was a stable one, and I went clean off the rails."

That was the hardest thing. She had let her father down.

"But you'd love Emmie," she said. "I'm not certain, but she seems to have your knack for getting what she wants." Her breath was deep as she drew it in. "And I'm finally stumbling out of the wilderness. I won't let you down anymore. But I wish you were here," she said. "I met a man I fell in love with. You'd really like him, I know you would. You'd say he was full of crap and molasses, and that's what you often said got you past your competitors.''

She spun his chair to look out the window to the grounds below. ''I'm sorry to admit I was too afraid to do anything about it.''

A truck moved up to the monitored gate. She leaned forward, watching to see if the housekeeper would buzz for the truck to enter. The truck doors opened, and three men got out, staring over the wrought-iron security gate at the house.

One of them was wearing jeans with one leg missing. Like Frisco.

Frisco. She jumped to her feet, and went tearing down the spiral staircase. ''Open the gate, Mrs. Dawson! Open the gate!''

And then she flew outside, across the wide lawn, making it to the gate just as it opened wide enough for her to run through and jump into Frisco's arms.

He kissed her on the mouth, and she hung on in a manner that would make any rodeo rider proud. Way past eight seconds.

And then slowly he put her down.

''Well, that was worth the drive,'' Tex said.

''A plus,'' Last said, ''If you ask me.''

Which no one did.

She gazed into Frisco's eyes, unable to stop holding his hands. ''I can't believe you're here.''

''Next time you decide to roll, could you at least

leave a trail of bread crumbs? I was scared to death I wouldn't find you."

Annabelle smiled. "I'm home now. No more rolling."

Frisco looked up at the big house. "Well, it's impressive and all, but too big for one woman and one tiny baby."

"Oh? What do you think I should do about that?"

"We could spend the night here," Last suggested. "I think I see a golf course out back. A big, snakey looking one with dog legs and tricky rough. I've always wanted to play on a course like that."

"Shh," Tex said, knuckling him. "Go get back in the truck."

"What I think is that we should develop our friendship," Frisco said to Annabelle, ignoring his brothers' conversation.

Slowly, he edged down, his bad leg bending to the side, so that he could rest on one knee. Annabelle held his hand tightly, trying to help support him, her heart blooming so big she didn't think she could breathe.

"I'd like you to be my best friend, Annabelle Turnberry, in all moments in our lives, good, bad and ugly. Through ice storms, broken limbs, Never Lonely Cut-n-Gurls and babies who cry in the night." He stared up at her, with love in his dark-brown eyes. "But mostly, I'm asking you to be my wife, because I love you, and goodness knows, you and Emmie grabbed my heart right out of my chest when I wasn't looking and I'm praying you'll keep it. And me.''

"Awkward, but the best he could do," Last whispered to Tex. "For a man unused to expressing himself, he's doing all right, doncha think?''

"Shh," Tex said. "I can't hear.''

But there was nothing else to hear, because Annabelle got down on her knees and whispered something for Frisco's ears alone, and then she slowly helped him to his feet. She fitted herself up under his arm, and supporting him, they walked through Turnberry's monitored gate.

Frisco reached out as they passed the brick columns supporting the gate and pushed a button, never looking back. The gate slid shut behind them.

"Hey! What about us?" Last called. "What about the golf course?''

Laredo laughed. Tex pulled his younger sibling away from the fence.

"That was the point," Laredo said. "They just left us behind. Be happy, bro," he said to Frisco with a last glance at the big house. "You and Annabelle and Emmie deserve that happy-ever-after.''

ANNABELLE LAUGHED AS Frisco tried to carry her over the threshold. "You're going to hurt yourself.''

"I'm not. I'm a big, tough, strong cowboy.''

"I love my big, tough, strong cowboy.''

"And I love you, whoever you were, are and turn out to be."

For a woman who had just discovered who she was in life, his words were powerful. "You have no idea how much you mean to me, Frisco Joe Jefferson."

They kissed, long and sweetly—until they heard Emmie let out a little cry.

"She must know you're here," Annabelle said with a smile.

"True happiness is when a man walks in the house to have his wife and daughter cry out for him," Frisco said, putting his arm around her. "Take me to my demanding daughter—and then we're going to have a treasure hunt. How many rooms does this shack have?"

"I don't know. More than twenty," she said, laughing at the meaningful expression on his face. "Why?"

"Can you count to twenty, Annabelle?"

"If you give me a week," she said, leaning up against him, her heart full of happiness.

"I'm giving you a lifetime."

Annabelle turned to look up at her father's portrait in the stairwell. "See, Dad? I told you you'd like him. Crap and molasses. Big promises, sweet talk and sticking power."

The recipe for success.

Epilogue

Annabelle smiled at her husband as he lay in a hammock on the grounds of the Turnberry estate. Emmie snoozed in the hammock beside him, which made Annabelle's heart warm in every corner. "I worried that you'd have trouble settling in here, Frisco. I was so afraid you'd miss your brothers. And Malfunction Junction."

"Worry not, lady love." Without joggling Emmie, Frisco snagged his wife, pulling her down on top of him. He kissed her, slow and long.

It had only been a month since the wedding, but every time Frisco grabbed Annabelle and kissed her like this, Annabelle felt certain no woman was as lucky as she. "You make me tingle all over," she told him.

"Then I'm not doing something right. You should be feeling sparks, lady. That's what I feel when you walk into a room. And I don't even want to put a name to what I feel when you walk into a room naked.''

She laughed. "Have I done that?"

"Not often enough. But we've got plenty of time. And I'm a very patient man. I'll be around for any nudity twitches you suddenly develop."

She smiled up at him. "And if I don't?"

He kissed her forehead and then her lips. "I know how to work a zipper. Buttons, bra straps, none of that can stand in the way of a man determined to hold his beloved."

"Am I? Your beloved?" she asked, knowing full well the answer but wanting to hear it anyway.

"Nah," he said.

She giggled. "Frisco!"

"Kiss me and maybe I'll rethink that."

She kissed the teasing smile right off his face.

"Wow," he said when they finally pulled apart. "You're my beloved and then some!"

"Did you feel sparks?" she whispered.

"I felt sparks, and I felt magic, and I felt love, Annabelle. I love you so much."

Frisco laid Annabelle's head on his chest. Quietly the three of them swung in the hammock, enjoying the gentle breeze. The warm afternoon sun. The happiness and peace of being together.

And being in love.

You were right, Dad, Frisco thought, closing his

eyes as he held his new family. Home is what a man feels in his heart.

And Frisco's home was with Annabelle.

* * * * *

Turn the page for a sneak preview of
LAREDO'S SASSY SWEETHEART
(HAR981)
the next book in Tina Leonard's miniseries
COWBOYS BY THE DOZEN
Available August 2003.

Chapter One

Laredo Jefferson had seen a lot of madness in the last month. Mimi had become engaged, a startling situation in itself. Frisco had married a fine woman, another surprising development. But he wasn't about to be caught in the same net. After all the years of drought on their ranch, they'd had a veritable shower of female charms visiting, and it was all he could do to resist paying court to every one of them!

Which got him thinking about traveling east—something he'd been thinking about long before the madness of love had hit the ranch. He was in the mood for adventure, a change of pace—not the madness of love. It's not going to hit me, he vowed, and picked up his packed duffel bag. He wasn't about to settle down.

He wanted to do something big.

Without another glance back, he left the only home he'd ever known to venture out into the cold March morning. First stop: Paying a visit to the

Lonely Hearts Salon, just long enough to say hello to some ladies who'd made his life a little more fun last month. *There* was a place for a troubled man to find a sympathetic ear.

Three hours later, he was standing outside the salon, amazed by the hubbub inside when suddenly the door flung open. His shirt collar firmly grasped in two desperate female hands, he was hauled inside.

He well remembered Katy Goodnight, who had him in her determined grip. He remembered thinking that a man could spend many good nights with a girl like her.

"This is him!" Katy announced to the room at large, which was filled with elderly men and a lot of women and even a chicken on one of the sink counters. "This is the man we can enter in the rodeo as the champion for Lonely Hearts, Texas. If anyone can ride Bloodthirsty Black, it's Laredo Jefferson. Ladies and gentlemen, pay homage to your champion, and the man who can whup the daylights out of our rival, the Never Lonely Cut-n-Gurls and their bull, Bad-Ass Blue!"

Voices huzzahed, hands clapped, Katy released his shirt so she could clap, too, and even the chicken uttered a startled squawk. But no one was more startled than Laredo. He wasn't a bull-riding savior.

He'd never ridden a bull in his life.

Katy whispered, "You got here just in the nick of time. You're my hero!"

He swallowed and decided to keep his mouth shut. After all, he'd been looking for a little adventure—and it wasn't every day a man got to be a hero to a woman named Goodnight.

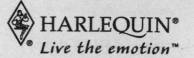